THE NEW BIZARRO AUTHOR SERIES
PRESENTS

# THE FLESH MOLDER'S LOVE SONG

## ROLAND BLACKBURN

ERASERHEAD PRESS
PORTLAND, OREGON

ERASERHEAD PRESS
P.O. BOX 10065
PORTLAND, OR 97296

www.eraserheadpress.com
facebook/eraserheadpress

ISBN: 978-1-62105-258-6
Copyright © 2018 by Roland Blackburn
Cover design copyright © 2018 Eraserhead Press

Printed in the USA.

# SKIN DEEP

A lot of the nurses told him that his aunt looked so peaceful lying there. Rain thought that was so much shit.

Take the blue tube that snaked its way down her throat. The off-blue smock that lent a greenish tinge to her skin like an aging reptile. The wires spiderwebbing their way from the bank of humming, beeping, squawking machines, turning her into nothing more than a medical marionette.

He knew what she had been, and in a way that made it worse. The chemo had taken her hair, even her eyebrows. Aunt Lucy had been a small force of nature, but the thing growing inside had shriveled her down into a small puppet that lay beneath the turquoise blanket.

When he'd come before, she'd held his hand in hers. *I'm on my way out,* she'd whispered. *You've got to find someone else, Rain. Someone who can make you happy.*

It had been a theme for years now. She'd raised him on romantic comedies, random coincidences and unusual changes of heart leading to that last kiss and riding off into the sunset. *When Harry Met Sally. Bridget Jones's Diary. Love Actually.* Even years after he'd left home for good, they'd gotten together every week for another movie night. *10 Things I Hate About You. Sleepless in Seattle. Pretty Woman.* For such a tough woman, Lucy had the most bizarre soft spot for love. She'd always told him that everything would work out all right in the end.

Now she hadn't spoken in days. If it wasn't for the incessant chirping of the machines, you'd even never know she was alive.

Rain watched the breather rise and fall, white plastic skittering towards the top of the tube and plummeting back down in a never-ending suicide. If he let his mind wander, sometimes the worst would appear, but even if permanently comatose, euthanasia would never be what she wanted. Aunt Lucy had been so Catholic she'd set a plate for the Pope at supper.

Besides, everything would work out all right in the end. Right?

He visited every couple of days, but this last week since the stroke had been the hardest. There was no speech, just the barest recognition in her eyes. The last two times he'd been there she hadn't even woken up, which was threatening to break his heart. Aunt Lucy was all the family he had left.

Rain heard the familiar warning tap out on the door. Visiting hours were over, and he leaned towards Aunt Lucy and kissed her on the forehead before heading back to the garage. It was like sandpaper against his lips.

When the elevator opened, Rain checked the painted pillar for his row number before hurrying onwards. His memory was spotty at best, but he thought with a reasonable amount of certainty that he was at least on the right floor of the parking garage. Entombed in underground concrete, the temperature outside was at least twenty degrees from the warmth of the hospital.

Rain tried not to think about what the nurse had told him right before he'd left.

The contrast between the immaculate high-tech hospital and piss-soaked parking garage never failed to impress him. Here the scattered bulbs hung sporadically in wire cages, at least half of them not working, rainwater or what he hoped was rainwater pooling beneath them in dark puddles. The walls were slowly accumulating a patchwork fuzz of rot green mold.

His footfalls were blows on a coffin lid, that special kind of echo reserved for vacant spaces and haunted houses. Rain pulled out his cellphone and clicked on the flashlight function, figuring that it couldn't hurt. Deep pools of shadow sloped and bled between pillars, and he figured the chances of missing his car entirely were about three to one. Twenty years old, the Nissan was held together mostly by sheer force of will as long as he didn't push it outside of a twenty mile radius. The peeling paint almost functioned as a bumper sticker.

Rain had seen this particular nurse almost two dozen times since his aunt's admittance. She was hard to miss. A lean dark presence with a shaved head and phenomenal skin, they'd developed a nodding relationship not uncommon to people meeting each other in a sterile professional setting. He'd been surprised, then, when the nurse had followed him back to her station and pulled him aside. Leaning close, she'd whispered nine knives into his chest.

Her name tag had read Masami. He'd never thought to ask for her name before.

He passed the next three pillars and paused next to the fading 2D, feeling that moronic vacancy reserved for those expecting to see their cars and finding an empty parking spot. The thought that anyone would have stolen it in a garage full of BMWs and Mercedes was absurd, although the idea that it might have spontaneously combusted didn't feel like a stretch.

Rain pressed on, confident now that he'd misremembered. He followed the ramp through patches of darkness down to the third floor and worked his way back to the elevator. This seemed more familiar, or at least the long black stretch with three broken bulbs like missing teeth did.

She'd put her hand on his arm, surprising him with the warmth and strength of her grip. Her eyes had been apologetic pools, and the sympathy from a near stranger brought a choking heat to his chest. With some absurdity he realized that they were close enough to kiss.

*It won't be long. You should make your peace.*

He thought he could make out the Nissan's silhouette, two spaces away from a beaten pickup and three down from a scarred pale van, and he quickened his pace. Dimly he was aware of a warmth in his cheeks, the wetness of every blink.

*Life is pointless. Death inevitable.*
*Organic computers, programmed to decay.*
*All we are is meat. All we are is flesh.*

The mantra reversed itself, alternated, suggested apocalyptic futility with the inevitability of a true earworm.

It was no surprise he didn't see the man coming.

A second pair of footsteps scraped echoes in the darkness behind him. A faint click came from the puddle of night, and when Rain turned the man emerged from the shadows behind the pillar, his faded blue jacket an almost pleasing contrast against the chipped paint of 3C.

He had a gun, Rain saw with no particular alarm. It was strange, but now his thoughts seemed to be coming from a far distance, as if they'd been fastened to a balloon and then played out into the whirling cosmos. They were being battered by a solar storm, but down along the string all he could feel were the barest tremors.

It wasn't hard to guess the stranger's intentions. He shouted something as he jerked himself forward, counting on surprise and intimidation to grease the transaction. Rain felt himself lifted off his feet, slammed into the side of the Nissan. Something crunched beneath him, and he hoped he hadn't just killed his passenger side mirror.

*All we are is flesh.*

The gun was in his face now, a cold black insect threatening to sting. Rain felt himself thud back into the Nissan again, his ass scraping against the glass. For some reason he was taken with the smoothness of his assailant's face, that he'd taken the time to shave before this.

*All we are is meat.*

There was a pause, and then a blinding flash of light erupted behind Rain's eyes. He sagged to his knees, aware that his temple had borne a whip from the butt of the pistol. The man's eyes were cold beads, his skin pale and sweating. *Why doesn't he just rob me? Take my wallet and go?* the balloon version of Rain asked. Down on earth, Rain could only shrug as the man drew back and hit him again.

*Flesh we all are.*

Something warm and red was seeping into Rain's eyes. He was aware that he was laughing.

What a fucking world. What a fucking world where your parents are snatched away by a semi on an icy road, where you bounce around the feral group home system for a while, when the aunt who manages to clear the board for adoption gets the big C six years in and, fight as she might, slowly gets eaten alive. What a fucking world where your dreams and your hopes are replaced by an office hamster mill and never-ending email chains.

What a fucking joke.

*Meat we all are.*

His laugh wasn't the response the assailant was looking for, who punctuated the good humor with a couple of swift kicks to his ribs. Rain wanted to say he wasn't laughing at him, but he really didn't think it would help.

The man leaned down. He was handsome, really, in a little-too-caveman kind of way. Lifting the pistol to Rain's cheek, he said something Rain couldn't quite make out. Rain's hand batted and clasped against his, a feeble butterfly trying to land.

*Flesh.*

*Meat.*

*Flesh.*

*Meat.*

What happened next Rain could never quite describe.

There was a warm rushing feeling, like his bladder letting go, as a pouring sensation erupted from his fingertips that quickly began to burn. Taken aback, at first the man didn't say anything, and they both just watched as the man's gun hand slowly began to reknit.

Fingers jellied and pooled together into a meaty knob, bones floating in continental drift, until his hand was a pink and shiny globe from which the barrel of the gun protruded like a black skyscraper.

Then the man began to howl, a long sharp bark of pain. Rain watched indifferently as the man's arm began to shrink and melt beneath his skin, collapsing into the warm wet orb which swelled and grew towards his heart, absorbing his wrist, forearm, elbow. By the time it split his coat sleeve in a loud farting rip, the red mass was roughly the size of a basketball.

There was blood, but less of it than one would think. The man gibbered and pleaded, all nonsense words now. Rain didn't withdraw his hand.

Something the size of a library globe now protruded from his assailant's right shoulder, as if he'd suddenly sprouted a veiny hydrocephalic head. The man's eyes bulged either in horror or from the pressure as his skin began to run, a boneless flood of grease that brought him to his knees as the deluge of meat poured to join the swelling globe. Phalanges separated and swam like rats escaping a burning ship. His other hand became an empty glove of skin, the meat swelling and buckling towards the core. The man's shoes slipped off with a rubbery thud.

"Please," the man said. Throughout their whole encounter, it was the only word Rain ever heard him say.

It didn't matter. He couldn't stop if he wanted to.

The stranger was the size of a large playground ball now, a grotesque pink mass that bulged and twitched with every heartbeat. What remained of his torso stuck out below it like a candy bar in a wad of gum, inexorably being drawn into the center, melting down to join the sphere.

His face, unmercifully, was the last thing to go. Corneas erupted and ran, the man's features red taffy that stretched and melted and puttied down his chin, flowing in gory waves to pool on the surface of this new thing. In the end all that was left a crimson planet, a sphere of pulsing horror that wept red tears on the asphalt.

There was nothing to suggest it had ever been human. That it had ever been a man.

Rain removed his hand. All at once he missed the warmth.

Then he threw up. Everything he had, seemingly everything he had ever eaten pooled steaming by the concrete wall. His head pounded as his stomach roiled, and Rain was pretty sure that he needed stitches.

Staggering, he slid himself behind the wheel of the Nissan, trying not to look at the gory orb now dripping on the pavement.

As he pulled away, he thought he saw it begin to roll.

Sitting in his tiny cubicle, Rain was pretty sure that he was dying.

He'd woken up with a black eye and a raging headache, his cheek and scalp sticky with dried blood. Decker had tried to lick him clean, happy dog kisses a mixture of halitosis and drool before his little rescue terrier had bounced off him gleefully, aware that breakfast was less than five minutes away. Rain groaned and stumbled his way to the bathroom mirror.

He felt worse than he looked, which was a testament

to how shitty everything really was. After Rain had washed off and gingerly probed the torn edges of the wound, he'd mitigated the damage as best he could with three extra-strength migraine pills and a glass of orange juice. When he'd glanced over at the clock, he wasn't surprised to see his alarm hadn't gone off, leaving him already fifteen minutes late for his shift at EpiCo.

Calling out was not an option. He'd already burned through most of his sick time for the year staying at the hospital.

Throwing himself together with what little resources he had left, Rain hurried through his routine, filled Decker's bowl with brown cereal, and then tried not to lose his mind in the Nissan for the thirty minutes it took him to drive the nine miles to the office. It had been built by the airport landing strip, directly below the National Guard's flight path. EpiCo had gotten a great deal on the property, most likely because it vibrated wildly every five minutes as jet engines threatened to tear its roof off.

Now he eyed his workstation balefully, trying to ignore the pounding behind his eyes and the swell of nausea rising from his stomach. The glow of the monitor was piercing, and he tried to distract himself from the monotony of entering numbers onto an Excel spreadsheet. It was mindless, data-entry work that at best would leave him starving the moment someone created better visual recognition software, but at least the files kept coming. The numbers kept adding up.

If he raised his elbows to either side, he could touch the walls. The morale boost from this was not sublime.

Rain had no clue what had happened the night before. Obviously someone had hit him hard enough to leave some pretty fucked-up marks, but his wallet hadn't been taken. Maybe the assailant had chickened out or got spooked by a security guard after the first couple of hits, though this didn't explain him driving home with a major head injury.

For some reason he kept thinking of dumplings. He wasn't quite sure why.

In the middle of flapping his elbows against the cheap fabric borders, he knocked the top file off his stack. It fell and yawned uselessly against the drab carpet like an awful bloom.

He reached down to get it without thinking and felt something tear. It was a ripping, excruciating pain, like the tendons were tearing free of his bones, and he bit back a cry as he snatched back his hand.

Holding it up to the light, Rain regarded it dubiously. It wasn't one hundred percent, but he was pretty sure that the fingers of his left hand were suddenly longer than the right.

By noon, much of Rain's headache had subsided, and when Ronnie had come by for their semi-weekly lunch date down in the third floor break room, his thoughts had more or less returned to normal.

He'd looked at his hands every thirty seconds or so. They seemed to have resumed their more or less normal dimensions as they clacked over the budget black keyboard. Maybe it had been a trick of the light. Maybe it had been his overworked mind. Hell, it was probably the head trauma.

With his usual tact, he waited until Ronnie had tucked into his second sandwich before he held his hands out before him like a magician asking the cops not to shoot. "Notice anything?"

Ronnie chewed thoughtfully, his wavy black hair slipping a lock down onto his forehead. He was a big guy who'd probably played defensive tackle in high school, but Rain didn't think he'd ever had the heart to hurt someone. It had probably cost him a ride at a state college, and now he was pushing three hundred pounds, trapped at a desk with his steer muscle slowly coagulating into fat. His eyes, though, were as bright as ever. "You forgot to paint your nails?"

"No, really. Look." When this failed to provide a gasp of wonder, he tried again. "Is one hand longer than the other?"

"Have you been huffing the white-out?" Ronnie raised

an eyebrow, then sighed. "Put 'em on the table."

Rain obliged him. To be fair, against the beige plastic they seemed normal, slightly asymmetrical hands. Ronnie shook his head. "Too many shots to the head at Fight Club last night, Wolfcastle. My abuelita warned me about you people."

The Wolfcastle name was stupid, as most office intrigue tended to be. Rain's parents had named him after the mountain in Washington, but all everyone ever remembered was the uber-German action star from the Simpsons. When they'd found out his name was Rainier, the Wolfcastle stuck right on the wall next to it. "I thought one was longer for some reason."

"Nope."

"Huh." Rain removed his hands from the table and stared at them for a moment. Nonplussed, Ronnie resumed his sandwich.

How bad was the cranial trauma?

He thought about it for a moment, how it had felt, the stretching—

"Fuck!" He almost kicked over his chair as a half-dozen bored drones swiveled their heads to mark him. His whole arm ached, with a burning, ripping sensation peeling down from his elbow, like his tendons had been scraped with razor wire.

When Rain didn't erupt into flames, the break room numbly turned back to lunch.

"Dude," Ronnie said. "You know profanity's only for management."

"Sorry," Rain murmured, then tried to address the room. "Sorry, everybody."

His hand still stung, and he glanced down at, wondering if he'd just crushed a wasp or been bitten by a brown recluse. These old buildings were prime targets—

There it was.

His fingers were an inch longer on his left hand.

This time he almost poked Ronnie in the eye in his rush

to throw them onto the table. "Okay, look. Look now."

"This again?" Ronnie worked on his sandwich and gave him a look that was one part pity, two parts confusion.

"No, look. One's longer, right?"

Ronnie shook his head, opened his mouth, and then shut it again. His gaze flickered from one to the other with the look of someone who's being burned by sleight of hand but isn't quite sure how the trick's being performed.

"Right?"

Ronnie shook his head, flapping that wavy black lock back across his forehead. "Look, it *appears*—"

That ripping sensation came again, and a pulse of liquid fire shot down his arm that brought tears to Rain's eyes. For some reason, though, it didn't hurt quite as badly this time. In fact, it almost felt, well—

"What the fuck?" Ronnie hissed. A couple of heads turned, but now that they had been labeled as the profane boys from processing, their five minutes of fame appeared to be up.

Rain looked down. His fingers were now three inches longer on his left hand, giving it the appearance of a pallid spider pulled from the bottom of the sea. He waggled them grotesquely, and the big man gave out a tiny shriek that was almost comical.

He thought about this. A giant hand, while slightly amusing, was probably not going to thrill his coworkers or win him any points with management. In fact, typing was going to be right out.

An ugly thought recurred, something familiar. Dumplings.

"What in the actual fuck?" Ronnie had grabbed his shoulder and tugged him closer like a rag doll. As Rain watched, his fingers shrank back, flesh and bone retreating to their original size. Ronnie turned to him with incredulity and more than a little horror. "How are you *fucking doing that*?"

"Profanity's only for management," Rain replied. He

twiddled his fingers. Nothing seemed out of place. In fact, he felt fantastic.

"How—?" Ronnie tried again, but the question appeared to stall out.

"This is going to sound crazy," Rain offered, trying to push away some very uncomfortable visuals of what he prayed was just a dream from the night before. "All the beating my head took might have given me some kind of power. Or something."

Ronnie was silent for almost a full minute. It was a feat usually only replicated when he was eating. Finally, he slid the remainder of his sandwich across the table and peeled back the top layer of bread. "That's stupid. Do the sandwich."

Obliging, Rain put his fingers on the cold slice of bologna, at once feeling a little stupid and godlike at the same time. He tried to make it expand, then lengthen, then wave. Nothing happened.

Rain jostled the slice, manipulated it, waved it around the room. For some reason, that burning sensation in his fingers wouldn't quite come. "Maybe it's the mustard."

Defeated, he handed the sandwich back to Ronnie, who considered it for a moment before shrugging and devouring the rest. "Damn," he said. "I was really hoping you could make my bologna bigger."


On his next break, he snuck downstairs and inspected himself in the dim bathroom of the second floor. It was dingy and ill-kempt, a holdover from when an active staff had occupied the space before it had been converted into storage and file retention after layoffs a couple of years ago. No one used it now except for bowel emergencies or recreational drug use. At this time of day, he had the whole chamber to himself.

Rain surveyed himself in the mirror, surprised he wasn't freaking out more. Stretchable hands—

*—you turned a person into a madball last night—*

—didn't seem to be, on the surface, that big of a deal. But what if that was only the tip of the iceberg? What if he could manipulate, well—everything?

He checked himself out again. Average looking guy, average build, average—well, that just about summed it up, didn't it? He was definitely more Steve Buscemi than John Cusack. No one was knocking down his door to star in their summer blockbusters. No one had asked him to ride horses shirtless on their calendars.

Raising a hand to his cheek, Rain let it rest there for a moment. What if he could change?

The familiar burning sensation came again, this time almost pleasantly warm. He relaxed, savoring it, letting it grow. An unbelievable calm began to settle in. When he glanced back at the mirror, he saw that his fingers were buried up to the first knuckle in his face.

Panic set in immediately.

There was no blood, which was a relief, but his stumps now protruded just below his cheekbone. Experimentally Rain flicked his tongue sideways. He caught the salty taste of his pinkie.

Revolted, he tried to yank his hand free. The pain was excruciating. Worse, his cheek didn't want to oblige. His face stretched, hanging in drooping ropes of tendon and pink flesh like taffy from his palm. A pattering of crimson sprayed the bowl of the sink and mirror. Rain realized he had exposed his jaw, the bone shockingly white and glistening. He could count every one of his teeth, and his tongue waggled like an obscene growth.

*Holy shit, I've deformed myself.*

He tried to press the loose remnants of his face back into place. The effect was less than ideal.

*Calm down. Calm down.*

Rain studied himself in the mirror, breath heaving in his

chest. He had gone from average to a wad of spent gum in less than sixty seconds.

*What am I going to do?*

Briefly, he envisioned never leaving the second floor. He could start a new life here among the files, haunting the rows and ghosting into EpiCo beneath a spectral half-mask. All he would need to survive was to plunder the vending machines every now and again and start bathing in the sink. In time, he would be a legend.

He patted at his face with both palms, fingertips massaging, that burning sensation back and bright as white phosphorus. It was at first both terrifying and strangely soothing. He tried to remind himself that this was his doing, that anything he could break he could also fix. This last he wasn't quite sure of, but his body seemed to be accepting the sentiment. A picture formed in his head, his mental image of himself, and after a while his hands began to comply. Eventually, the ropes began to fold back into the whole, the flesh patching over into smooth planes.

After a while, he dared to study himself in the mirror. To his surprise, Elm thought he looked more or less normal again, right down to the black eye, though he might have knocked half a point off his overall appearance. His skin showed no signs of stress or droopy elasticity. He wasn't even red.

The blood he cleaned up with paper towels and crammed into the waste bin. Despite company policy, he spent the rest of the day on the internet, scanning and then poring through DIY guides on sculpting. It was amazing how much practical information was out there.

Room 38 at the hospital was sterile, but just underneath that combination of chemicals and cycled air, Rain could smell the rot.

He sat by the window, watching his aunt's chest rise and

fall, still trying to come to terms with his nightmare-that-maybe-wasn't in the parking garage.

Parking in the same spot after work, the chipped paint of 3C marking his turf like an obelisk, he'd glanced around surreptitiously at the pavement. There was nothing there. No blood. No gobbets of flesh. Certainly not a mugger who had been melted into David Cronenberg's beach ball.

It would have been so easy to believe it had all been a dream. That he could now elongate his fingers or rip his face off was a solid vote in the other direction.

The machines chirped and hitched, never breaking rhythm. Rain got up and paced around, glancing down at his aunt on the bed. Her eyes were closed, blue tube snaking through the plastic mask that covered her lower jaw. A set of plastic strings protruded from her left wrist under pale scraps of tape. He couldn't help but think she would have hated this.

But when the x-rays and MRI's had all been revealed, cards flipped over in a shitty magic trick, they both had gone along with the chemo. The treatment had shriveled her, diminished her, but the blackness inside her had somehow only grown stronger. It could happen to anyone. Hell, often it did.

Rain rubbed absently at the gouge in his scalp where he'd been pistol-whipped, the crusty black scab somehow a relief beneath his fingers.

*Physician, heal thyself.*

The thought occurred to him unbidden, and Rain yanked his hand away, all too conscious of the sudden weight it had taken on. Not here.

Not here.

But if he could—

There was a gentle knock before the door swooshed open. Masami, came in, sparing him a strained smile as she checked first his aunt and then the machines.

She paused next to the respirator as if something had just occurred to her. "I don't make it a habit of getting too deep into other people's business."

It took Rain a moment to realize that she was speaking to him. He tucked his hand behind his back. "That's good?"

"What happened to your face?"

Rain tried to picture his cheek coming apart like bloody taffy. "Some guy kicked my ass in the parking garage. I think a security guard or something scared him off."

Her eyes went a little wider. They were remarkable, as green as a forest at dawn. "Here? Oh. Shit. Are you okay?"

"My pride took a bigger beating than my face, I guess."

She snapped her fingers. "That's why the detective was here."

"Detective?"

"Guy with the blue suit. Flashed something around, asked if anyone knew anything about some incident in the parking garage last night. Who was working, who was here late, all that."

"Did you say anything?" Rain wasn't sure why this was important, but for some reason he had to know.

Masami glanced behind her. "I don't talk to cops."

Nodding, Rain turned his attention back to his aunt, unable to shake the bad feeling that he knew exactly what had happened in the garage. Only— no one had reported it, had they?

The nurse took this as her cue. "I've got to finish my rounds, so I'll leave you to it. Visiting's over in five. One last thing?"

"What's that?"

"A little bruising suits you. You look better than you have in weeks."

# SUBCUTANEOUS

In the handicapped stall on EpiCo's second floor, Rain rolled up his sleeves. Ronnie glared at him with dubious mistrust.

It had been a hell of a week for Rainier, but he had dealt with it as gracefully as he'd thought was humanly possible. Despite the warnings from Masami, the other nurses, and the glib doctor who sometimes drifted through the room, Aunt Lucy clung to life with the pugnacious vitality she'd always shown badgering him back to his studies, sniffing him over for vodka fumes, or complaining about Hugh Grant in *Notting Hill*.

Stranger still, whatever it was that had happened to him hadn't faded away at all. For some reason, it had gotten stronger.

After the first dozen internet searches for other people with flesh sculpting powers (results: several fictional superheroes, plastic surgeons, and one televangelist), he had spent his nights plugging away at YouTube, WikiHow, and any other web pages showing tutorials on sculpting or shaping material. He'd taken a community college seminar that Saturday that had eaten a significant chunk out of his savings to work on clay models of the human form. On Sunday he'd dared his first library visit.

He had become interested in anatomy. Not because he thought he'd become a doctor, or even a semi-capable faith healer, but at some deeper level, he was already wondering what was possible.

Decker, he had to admit, had not been the most willing of guinea pigs, but the results had been nothing short of remarkable. He had already gone through two bags of peanut butter dog biscuits. When Rain had started, the burning sensation still took over, searing through synapse and sinew to flare into a desperate agony, but after a while—

It had never lessened. That couldn't be worked around. It still hurt like hell, but rather like a sampler of fine vintages, he had grown almost to appreciate it. In the meantime, Decker had sprouted floppy spines, vestigial wings, ropes of skin that could pass for tentacles. Confused, the terrier had eventually seemed fine with it, especially since Rain had painstakingly returned him to normalcy at the end of every session. If anything, his little puppy had probably gained four pounds worth of peanut butter.

Ronnie had held out for two hoagies before agreeing to follow him to the second-floor washroom. It wasn't that he was a mad binge eater, but he knew a bargain when one came his way. The first he'd eaten in the tiny break room and stuffed the other in the fridge, all the while warning Rain that HR and a substantial lawsuit were only a phone call away if his magic tricks involved making Rain's pants disappear.

Now, in the ill-lit stall, Rain found himself tingling with anticipation. If he could only—

But that was putting the cart into the middle of the interstate. He needed to slow down. "Give me your hand."

Ronnie raised an eyebrow. "No funny stuff?"

"Deadly serious. Come on."

Ronnie sighed and offered his forearm. Rain took it in both hands eagerly, and for the first time Ronnie began to look nervous. "What are you going to do?"

"Shhh." His fingers kneaded the big man's wrist. Rain visualized what he wanted, picturing it rising from the clay. Still nothing.

"What's supposed to happen?" Ronnie asked.

*Shit.* Maybe he couldn't do it when the other person was watching, though dumplings sprang to mind. Maybe if Ronnie hit him—

The big man laughed. "You've got one more minute before I need another sandwich."

"What?"

"Bathroom economy, amigo."

Frantically, Rain picked up the pace, his fingertips violently massaging Ronnie's thick wrist. The sandwich wasn't that big an issue, but he was already down twelve bucks and some dignity. He was nonplussed when the big man began counting down.

*All cells at the beginning are formless, without genetic markers or predestined codes*, Rain thought. *They can become anything. It's only a matter of making them remember.*

In his mind's eye, he saw it. The tissue moving, extending, swelling. Nature abhorred a vacuum. Rain only had to create one.

The fire began in his fingertips, wrenching upwards to his elbow. Rain moaned.

With a litany of curses, Ronnie tried to pull his wrist back. It could have been welded to Rain's fingers for all the good that did.

Bronze flesh raised and puckered below Rain's palm. His heart raced as he formed the growth, sculpting it with painstaking care. His friend watched with horrified fascination as it rose and began to take shape.

"Ah." He grunted. "Ah. Ah. Ah."

"Does it hurt?" Rain asked.

"No, dude. I'm practicing my affirmations. Of course it fucking hurts."

Ideas began to occur to Rain as the burning sensation began to peak, the myriad of options flitting through his consciousness. Tentacles and feathers, spines and beaks, stunted wings and carapaced pincers. Modifications so fantastic and bizarre they'd never even been dreamt of in the natural world. Was this what creation was like? How could one not go mad with the possibilities?

He pulled his hand back before ambition could truly take hold. Ronnie gasped in shocked incredulity.

It wasn't much. From the big man's wrist protruded a single strange nodule, no bigger than a golf ball. Ronnie poked at it gingerly. "That's gross."

Rain allowed himself to feel it. The jellied mass beneath the skin seemed to squirm beneath the pressure. It was, in fact, more than a little gross.

"Is that all you've got?" Ronnie examined his wrist, turning it this way and that beneath the yellow light. "Or can you make me, I don't know, grow an extra arm or something?"

Rain shrugged. "I don't know. Maybe."

"Like, can it can be more than this?" Ronnie nodded. "Because, if I can be frank, this isn't very copacetic. Does it work better on you? Can you give yourself a twelve-inch dong or something?"

Rain shrugged. "Maybe. Maybe it just works better for me now."

"Okay. Well, I believe you now, but this is kind of weird. Take it off."

He placed his fingers on Ronnie's growth, trying to ignore the sick heat that swam beneath them. Rain massaged it gently, willing it to change shape, to melt back into Ronnie's body into whatever it had been before.

Nothing happened, and Rain pushed harder, trying to drive his will like a chisel through a side of beef.

Nothing happened for a while longer. Ronnie checked his watch. "Lunch is almost over, amigo. Can you get rid of it or not?"

"Fuck. I'm sorry." Rain panted. "It doesn't want to go away right now."

The big man shook his head. "You owe me. What is my wife going to say?"

"You're not married."

"*Future* wife. When I meet her. Or him. I'm pretty open-minded at this late stage of the game." Ronnie pulled his arm away and tucked the shirtsleeve back over his wrist. If one wasn't paying attention, it could have been a very ostentatious watch. "Sandwiches. Every day until it's gone. And beers tonight. Plus you owe me one."

"That's fair." Rain was only half-listening as Ronnie slunk out of the bathroom stall, washed his hands, and exited through the file repository. There had been no issues with Decker, who had at several points this week appeared to be made entirely of canine Play-Doh. Why couldn't he take it back?

He had played with the fire for the rest of the day at EpiCo, alternating between entering columns of numbers into the computer with lengthening and shortening his limbs. The frustration at not being able to take away the growth was slowly giving way to curiosity. Ronnie only showed it to him from across the row of cubicles every fifteen minutes. By the end of the day he'd taped a sheet of paper to his arm with *DEATH NODULE* scrawled across it, a convenient arrow pointing to the target. Rain wondered if he was creating a hoagie monster.

After the first couple of lengthenings, he began to think he was onto something. If he stretched his fingers more than another foot below his desk, he began to feel a weird sense of draining, and it hadn't taken long to discover that this because his stomach had shrunken considerably. Not in a way that might prove ultimately attractive, either, but just diminished. The farther they stretched, and he had dared as much as three feet before worrying that if startled he'd have to whip them back into his body like a tape measure, the less his stomach became.

It made sense, after all. Everything had to come from somewhere.

Maybe, and it seemed likely, conservation of matter was in play. He couldn't create new flesh, add or subtract from what was at hand.

Like any sculptor with a block of clay, he could only mold.

"I think you're the Devil!"

Ronnie yelled this over the bustle of the sports bar, his wings a greasy pile of stained bones before him. The Blazers were playing on twenty of the twenty-four screens like an image seen through insect eyes and Rain was has having a hard time focusing between the bursts of cheering and groaning that exploded every fifteen seconds or so. It was like a schizophrenic Colosseum where no one could decide if they liked the lions.

He had stopped by the hospital to check on his aunt before heading out with Ronnie to the outskirts of downtown. She hadn't been awake when he stopped by, the streak now lasting more than a week, and she looked smaller than he could ever remember lying there beneath her blankets. Something was tearing inside him, an emotional rupture that he was having a harder and harder time trying to contain. Everything else regarding her condition was still more or less stable, a slow handcart to hell. Masami had given him a sad smile when he'd left.

On his way to the elevator, he'd noticed a put-together man in a dark suit hovering by the nurses' station, chatting up one of the night shift. For whatever reason, he'd turned around and slunk out through the far stairs.

A sportsman threw the ball to another sportsman, and

everyone groaned. Rain tried another sip of his beer, which tasted suspiciously like pine tar was the central ingredient.

"What?"

"Maybe not the Devil. But possibly a really lesser demon."

"I don't think that's fair."

"You've got magic fingers. It's weird." Ronnie finished his beer and waved another two into existence. The nodule on his wrist, Rain noticed, hadn't increased in size, which was a small relief. He had been trying to brainstorm why it wouldn't come off for most of the afternoon with little to show for it. "Can I ask you something?"

Rain shrugged. "If I can answer it."

The big man swiveled on his barstool, surveying the half-full room with a proprietary air. "Look around you. Who in this room would you most want to hook up with tonight?"

"What?" An embarrassed flush crept up behind his cheeks. If he had listed the top ten possible things a man with a massive growth would want to talk about, this wouldn't have made the list.

The big man gazed at him from beneath his heavy brow. "Don't be such a prude. It's just a question. There's no right answer."

"I'm not really thinking about that right now." And he hadn't been. His last relationship had lasted four weeks before calmly disintegrating from some light ghosting into the eventual full seance, and that had been over two years ago. Once Aunt Lucy had gotten sick, his love life had drifted into a mental storage closet and he'd been giving the monks a run for their money. He had thought he'd try to take that part of himself out again when everything was over, but right now he had more than enough emotional scissors to run with.

"And that's what's wrong with you." Ronnie banged his hammy fist on the bar for emphasis, and several of the nearer customers jumped. It was an inevitable reaction when a man the size of a small bull waved anything. "You've told me about your aunt before, but you can't just dry up and blow away in the meantime. Is that what she would have wanted?"

She'd have wanted him to find his Meg Ryan. Aunt Lucy had asked him if he was seeing anyone or when he was planning to settle down at every movie night before, and a pang of guilt shot through him that felt at once stupid and very real.

Rain shook his head, and Ronnie seemed to take that as absolution. "So look. Be cool, but look. And tell me."

The thought that Ronnie might be coming onto him occurred and then quickly dissipated. Three-fourths of the patrons around them were clad in black and red jersey shirts and jeans, but there were a few who either didn't like basketball, conformity, or both. Rain looked around, a little dumbfounded. "I don't know."

"That's your problem." Ronnie pounded the bar again, and Rain began to wonder if the chicken grease was going to his head. "You're a man, mijo. You've got to be thinking about these things."

Rain tried for another sip of his beer and, to his surprise, found it empty. "Yeah?"

"I'm trying all the time," Ronnie patted his massive chest and slid him the second glass. "Big guy like me can crush my enemies and allies alike, but that doesn't stop me. The way I see it, you walk into a room. Three-quarters of the people aren't going to be attracted to you. That's just the way it is: you're too tall, too short, too heavy, too lean, hair's stupid, hair's not stupid enough. Pure biology. Ain't nothing you can do to change it, so no point sweating it. Less point in chasing it."

Rain was appalled to find himself following along. "Okay."

"That leaves you with a quarter of the room, now, which might have limited interest. You might physically fall into their parameters, which then starts the psychological round. Are you too serious? Is everything a joke? Are you some kind of asshole? Or not nasty enough?"

"I'm listening." And he was. That Ronnie had a fully-developed dating philosophy seemed no less unusual than anything else that had happened in the last two weeks.

"My point is that you're already down to twenty-five percent. Through a couple minutes of human interaction, you'll shave off another twenty." Ronnie put his hand down again for emphasis. "And what does that leave you with?"

"Just five."

"Just?" The big man looked incredulous. "That means that if you're don't try to be something you're not, one out of every twenty people are going to be interested. There's nothing as liberating as that."

"This might be the beer talking," Rain said. "But that actually made some cogent sense."

"Right?" Ronnie finished his third beer, and waved over another. "I mean, mileage may vary, but hey. The problem is, you're in a position to change all that."

"Problem?"

"There's a rumor going around the office. That you're either wearing make-up, or got some light plastic surgery. Some people think it's both."

Rain almost spat pine tar. "What?"

The big man put his hands up in mock defense. "Whoa, whoa, amigo. I'm just the messenger. A lot of the catty guys in HR were talking about it. Not true, right?"

"No." The very idea of it was absurd.

"Okay, okay. Thing is, you're prettier than you were last week."

"What?" It was his third in five minutes, and he really shouldn't be as easily surprised, but there was no other reaction. Every time he settled into Ronnie's lane, the truck jumped the median.

"Don't worry. This isn't me hitting on you. I'm just

comfortable enough in my sexuality to rate the appearances of other men. You've been about a five the entire time I've known you, but since you started stretching your hands, you've become more of a Portland eight. Do you keep melting your face off?"

"No." But Ronnie was making him wonder, all right. If he could change the shape of his body, was it something he was just doing subconsciously? Knitting together a whole new version?

"You don't have to get weird about it." Ronnie took another swig from his beer, and the bar erupted into mad cheers as someone threw a ball somewhere on the row of screens. "I'm just saying, my whole schematic? Fuck those numbers when you're one of the beautiful people. That brunette?"

Rain followed his gaze to a nubile figure in jeans and a Greg Oden jersey tee that hugged her figure like a second skin. He had to admit, it wasn't the easiest thing to look away.

Ronnie pressed on. "She could have almost any man in this bar if she wanted to, but that's really not that amazing. Men are dogs. But she could probably wrangle her way home with half the ladies too. The Asian girl by the pinball machine? Same story. If you're pretty, the rules get thrown out the window, amigo."

"I'm not sure what you're getting at." His head swam. Rain looked down and found that he had somehow fought his way through four beers. His tongue felt like the inside of a mop bucket.

"Meaning that could be you, mijo. If you're going to change your appearance, fuck this half-measure shit. Go all the way."

Rain nodded. He felt surprisingly good, the alcohol trading out his general depression for a low optimism that he'd pay for tomorrow. "You think I should become a woman?"

"What? No. I mean, unless you want to. It's a golden age, but what I'm saying is that you don't have to settle for just becoming marginally more attractive. You can be one of them. A pretty boy. One of the beautiful people."

"Yeah?"

"Yeah. And then I can live vicariously through you."

"Maybe. But you shouldn't keep talking about—" Rain felt around for words but came up empty. "—what I can do."

"Mijo, you've got nothing to worry about. Just live a little, all right?"

"Yeah?"

"Bartender," Ronnie called out. "Get my man some shots!"


His phone blared from somewhere in the room.

He heard it chirping through a groggy haze, emerging slowly from his cave of sleep to hiss balefully at the rays of actual consciousness. Rain's head hurt the very second he tried to move, and his mouth felt like boiled sandpaper. Flailing, his hand slapped the end table a series of futile blows. Where the hell was it?

Something shifted next to him, a soft warmth pressing against his leg. He heard a *thunk* come from the other side of the room, and then the chirping was mercifully gone.

Settling back down into the pillow, he tried to sink into merciful death. The soft warmth against his leg became more insistent.

It wasn't unpleasant, but he tried to will it away all the same. The pounding in his temples was a blacksmiths' chorus.

A weight detached itself from the other side of the bed and the mattress rebalanced. Footsteps padded out to the small bathroom. The door shut, and after a moment the toilet flushed. He had a feeling these events bore some minor significance, though his aching head was having trouble putting that entirely into sequence.

The footfalls drew nearer, and something made a dull *clunk* as it was placed on his end table. Rain chanced stabbing pain to crack an eye.

The brunette from the bar was staring down at him with

a mix of morbid curiosity and amusement. She was also, Rain noticed, completely nude.

She caught his eyes widening. The groan of pain it elicited made her laugh. "Not that it's my business, but it looks like you either have to call out or crawl your ass to work, big guy."

*Big guy?* That didn't sound right.

The brunette turned and began searching the floor with the unselfconscious air of someone who was used to being stared at. Her body was exquisitely proportioned, from the swell of her breasts to the curve of her calves, and Rain wondered how much work went into maintaining that look. Not that he was complaining.

Rain felt lightheaded as a familiar rush of blood vacated his brain. It was the kind of thing glam bands had written anthems about.

She fished her panties off the carpet and slipped them on before catching him still gawking. The brunette gave him a wry grin and traced her gaze to his swelling beneath the sheet. "We don't have time, cowboy. Both of us have got to go."

For a moment she seemed to reconsider, then stuck out her hand. Her breasts bounced as they shook, and between the pain and arousal Rain thought his head might explode. "Kimmie."

"Rain."

"Oh, I remember who *you* are." She found her Blazers shirt and pulled it down over her head before fishing her jeans out of the corner and tugging them over her hips. "I think we both a got a little too crazy last night. Seriously, though. You've got to get moving if you're going to get to work."

The brunette slipped out of the bedroom, and he heard her footsteps track down the narrow hall of the apartment. A short bark, a coo of approval, and he knew she'd met Decker.

Decker. Oh, shit. How normal was Decker right now?

His door creaked open, and Kimmie backed up into the room as Decker trotted in after her. He was, Rain saw, mercifully just a terrier.

Kimmie set a cup of water and three aspirin down on the end table and smiled. "We've all got to play hurt sometimes."

She squatted down onto the carpet and rubbed Decker behind the ears, oblivious to the mind-boggling display of her profile. Rain made another groaning sound and flung his feet onto the floor, kicking the sheet off with mild annoyance.

Kimmie whistled with a wry grin. "Did I do that?"

He looked down at himself for the first time, really looked. He thought he might be going insane.

Muscles stood out on his torso in stark, veiny relief. He hadn't just bulked up, but become as ripped as humanly possible. Every abdominal pressed against his skin as if it were trying to escape. His chest and shoulders were thick with sinew, thighs and calves now hammers.

Of course, he hadn't stopped there.

He'd given himself a giant dick.

It was this that bobbed and waved, a python bigger than a paper towel roll. *Fuck. It's no wonder I can't think straight. I've got no fucking blood for anything else.*

He gazed stupidly at the water and the aspirin for a moment before scooping them up and downing them. Something knotted in his stomach for a moment that meant trouble later, but he pushed it away.

Kimmie leaned over and kissed his forehead chastely. "I've got to go. You should take care of that, big guy."

She flicked his erection, causing a shrill yelp, and slipped out the door with a giggle.

Decker whined from somewhere at the foot of the bed. Between waves of nausea and a grinding between his temples, not for the last time that day Rain wondered just what the hell he'd done.

Row after row of numbers drifted by on the screen. It was kind of relaxing, which was good because he'd already thrown up twice and taken enough acetaminophen to immolate his liver. Apparently simply willing a massive hangover away was beyond the scope of his power.

He'd worn long sleeves to work, not entirely sure what to do about the leaner, meaner him. That he'd thought it a good idea to resculpt his entire body worried him, and he wasn't entirely sure how to turn it back. Muscles, flab away?

Not that he was sure he wanted to. Despite the obvious risks, it had worked. He'd achieved a body that frankly would have taken hundreds of hours and a thousand fewer microwave burritos to obtain. Sure, people that knew him might gawk at the sudden transformation, but he thought he could conceal it for a little while and then casually name-drop a gym membership, transcendental meditation, and a keto diet.

The penis, though. There was no choice but to scale that back. Walking around had been an adventure, and after the second dizzy spell when he thought of the night before had almost sent him toppling through the water cooler, reducing himself to less than porn-star standards had become a medical necessity.

In between files, he studied medical websites, anatomy lessons. The body was a machine. A complex one, to be sure, but still a machine, with all the wires and fibers attendant. If he was going to keep altering it—

Ronnie drifted by for the third time in two hours. This time instead of exchanging a knowing wink he stopped. If he was any the worse for wear from the night before, he wasn't showing it. In fact, he almost glowed.

"So, how did your night go?" He waggled his eyebrows. It was horrible.

"From the brief scenes I remember, pretty well." Rain managed a tired smile. "I'm paying for it right now."

"Right? Right?" Ronnie waited. When nothing else was forthcoming, he sighed. "Living vicariously through you, remember?"

"What? Sorry." Rain felt his phone vibrate against his thigh. "The shots were probably a bad idea. I don't remember much after that."

"You didn't drink any more than I did," Ronnie pouted. The fact that he was the size of two Rains flitted quickly by. "You should have said you were a lightweight, mijo, because she was *foooooine*."

"Yeah." The headache was back, a sharp icepick threatening his eyes.

"Are you going to see her again?"

"I don't know. I don't even think I got her number."

Ronnie clapped him on the back. It was uncomfortable. "Playah!"

"Yeah." Rain wondered if dissolving into a fine mist would help his current predicament. "What's going on, Ronnie?"

"What? Nothing, nothing." Ronnie looked behind him surreptitiously. "Except for one of those little favors you owe me. Maybe one of those."

"Favors. Plural?"

"I got you laid last night, amigo. Wingman extraordinaire. I think that qualifies me for a bonus."

Sighing, Rain drummed his fingers against the desk. The urge to lengthen them was palpable. "Bonus what?"

The big man's eyes darted again. "Not here. I'll see you downstairs in five minutes."

Ronnie ambled away like a ninja gone to seed. Rain sighed and ran through his numbers again. He was due for a break anyhow, though he'd rather not be seen following Ronnie to an abandoned restroom. Of such things, HR nightmares are born.

He pushed away from his desk and stood, keeping an eye out for his manager. Maneuvering through row after row of low cubicles and ignoring the dull ache in his stomach, he eventually made it to the small corridor, threw open the fire stairs, and descended the rough concrete steps to the second floor. There was something different down here, the air yellow and stale. It was disquieting, and he hurried to the old washroom without looking back.

"Amigo? That you?"

Ronnie was already sequestered in the ill-lit stall at the rear of the restroom. Rain slipped inside and closed the door behind him. "All right. What are we doing here, Ronnie?"

"You get to invite me to bathroom hookups, but not the other way around? That doesn't sound like friendship, mijo."

Rain rolled his eyes. "We've got fifteen minutes, and that's pushing it. What's up?"

"Don't be in such a hurry. This is a sensitive topic." Ronnie took a deep breath, then began unbuckling his pants.

Alarm bells went off in Rain's head immediately. "Hey now, buddy—"

"No, not like that. Look, I might have been a little less than honest with you last night." Ronnie let out the breath in a typhoon exhalation. "I don't do as well as maybe I let on. Trouble is, I'm a big big guy, right? But I lack confidence."

Rain stared at a wet patch on the ceiling and tried to imagine himself anywhere else. "Ronnie—"

"No, listen. It's because I've got all this muscle, but this little *pequeno pescado*."

"I don't think women care as much about that as you'd think."

"What, you speak for fifty percent of the population now? It's not about them, my friend." He tapped his temple. "It's about what's in here."

"That's what I'm trying to say. It's where your head is at—"

"Are you telling me you didn't?" His eyes were saucers, white and hopeful.

Rain paused. The wet patch on the ceiling loomed ever larger. *Fuck.* "What do you want me to do?"

"Give me something I can go to town with. Not like crazy, but like *macho*."

"I don't know if I can do that." He thought of dumplings, and shuddered. "I haven't really, well—changed anyone else. What if I fuck it up? Leave you with a pound of bratwurst or something?"

Ronnie put a hand on his shoulder. It was intensely disturbing. "I believe in you."

Sighing, Rain thought of the last uncomfortable qualifier. There was sadly no getting around it. "You know this means I probably have to touch you, right?"

Ronnie shrugged. "I've been to the doctor."

"And this is your favor, all right?" It felt important to clarify that. Rain was no prude and was all for everyone living their lives however they wanted, but frankly he didn't want to handle Ronnie's genitals any more than he wanted to be fisted by an octopus.

"Sure. Right."

Rain reached behind himself and then realized he'd probably be a better sculptor if he saw what he was doing. Ronnie was staring at him in wide-eyed wonder.

"No eye contact," Rain said.

"Okay." Was that disappointment he heard?

He closed his hand around Ronnie. The burning sensation began to spread from his fingertips to his wrist, an aching tear. In his mind he scrolled through some of the anatomy diagrams he'd checked out, trying to remember the vascular system, the corpus spongeium, the glans as he drew meat from elsewhere inside Ronnie and *shifted* it, molded it, altered it into what he needed.

Ronnie let out a low moan. Rain glanced up through gritted teeth. "Hurts," the big man said.

"Yeah." Creation often did. The thought frightened him a little, but he put it on the back burner.

Ronnie's dick began to lengthen, extending outwards and down like toothpaste from a tube. Rain resisted the urge to ask Ronnie to say *when* and pulled his hand away after thirty seconds or so. That pyretic feeling faded, replaced by a hint of uncomfortable cold.

The thing looked normal, in that it wasn't a grotesque mass or a third arm. "It's done."

The big man exhaled and looked down, taking himself in hand. "Hey now."

"Um." Rain had no idea how long they'd been down in the abandoned washroom, but wanted to wash his hands and be gone.

"Oh, yeah." Ronnie glanced up at him. "Amigo, you gotta go."

Room 38 was colder than normal. Beyond the whirring of the respirator and the electronic chirping of the machines, Rain listened to the footsteps in the hall, the traffic of life and death. He held his hands out in front of him and studied them, mind wandering, his heart pounding away.

Out of the blue he'd gotten a text from Kimmie, an invitation over to her place. He found it hard to believe, but there it was. Had he made that good of an impression as a drunken wreck? Come to think of it, he was pretty sure he hadn't even given her his number.

Rain had responded quickly, trying not to sound as desperate as he felt.

His aunt lay underneath the light blue sheets, automatons jutting from her arms beneath the fluorescent lights. Rain thought back to the abandoned stall, what he had done—

*Stop it.*

Ronnie had come back from the washroom with two thumbs up and a big dumb grin plastered across his face. If he could change other people—

*Stop it.*

Worlds apart. The two were worlds apart.

There was a knock on the door, and Masami slipped

into the room like a lean shadow in blue scrubs. She had moved over to the monitor and was checking the display before she suddenly froze.

*Oh, shit.* "Is it bad?" he asked.

She studied him critically, just barely biting her lower lip. "Steroids?"

"What?" He glanced down at himself. Veins pressed against his forearms like angry cords. "Oh, no. No. Just—eating better. Working out."

"You realize we see each other five times a week, right?" Her smile didn't quite reach her eyes. "Because, jeez. Not that I don't appreciate it, but if whatever you're doing is all natural, it's time to market that shit."

He tried a grin that didn't quite fit. "Maybe I will."

"Hah." She turned back to the monitor for a moment, checked the complex system of tubes and hoses protruding from his aunt. She played with her lower lip some more, mulling something over, and then addressed him again. Her eyes were the luscious green of a forest at dawn. "Look, I can't pretend that I understand what you're going through right now. She's the only family you have, and I can't imagine how hard it must be to come in here and sit in that chair every night. Your aunt's a fighter, but this is one she's not going to be able to win."

"It's natural to feel desperate. To feel like everything's out of your control."

She took a breath. "But you realize there are no shortcuts, right? Everything has a cost. Whatever you're doing to yourself, and that level of ripped is *not* normal, you're going to pay for it later." Masami took a deep breath. "That's it. End of speech. Just think about toning it down, all right?"

"Thanks," he said. "For caring. No drugs, but I'll try to dial down the body sculpting."

Her smile was genuine. "Okay. Now I know you're high."

The buzz from his pocket snapped the moment in half,

and Rain reached for it as the nurse went back to her duties. Kimmie had sent him a picture. Kimmie apparently believed that their text relationship was now clothes-optional.

"I've got to go," he announced, not exactly sure why.

Masami nodded. "Visiting hours are almost over anyhow. Good night."

"Thanks. You too."

"Try not to hulk out on your way to the parking garage."


The cold of the empty chamber hit him like a lead pipe the moment the doors opened. The faint smell of ammonia wafted in just after.

He hurried out into the concrete garage, mindful of the large puddle that had formed where the asphalt met the sidewalk. Since the night of the nightmare, Rain had tried to park closer on subsequent visits, but by the time he got there after work the parking garage was always almost full, with just a few open spots interspersed amongst the scattering of cars. Once more he'd had to settle for leaving the Nissan way out in the boonies.

An uncomfortable sense of deja vu was beginning to settle over him, and Rain checked the lettering on the pillar just to make sure he hadn't gotten lost again.

Peering into the darkness, he could just make out the Nissan amongst the other cars, squatting beneath one of the only surviving bulbs. His breath clouded out before him, and he took long, purposeful strides, trying not to think of dumplings and failing.

He could go straight to Kimmie's, he thought. He'd left enough food out for Decker—

"Rainier? Rainier Sorley?"

He glanced around, but saw no one. First superpowers, now voices. It was almost a relief, he thought sadly, the inevitable consequence of going mad.

"Mr. Sorley?"

A man stepped out of the dark patch behind D4. He didn't move so much as materialize.

That sense of panic grew stronger. Rain glanced over his shoulder at the elevator. He still might be able to make it in time.

Maybe not, though. This guy was big, and as he approached he raised his hand, letting the brown leather case in it flap open. Something golden glinted in the dingy light. "Detective Jacoby."

The stranger was balding, with a head that simply melted into his shoulders without a conventional neck. His torso was broad beneath his dark suit jacket, a shade of blue so black it was almost indistinguishable. The man's tie was matching and immaculate.

Rain didn't bother to answer. Too late for the elevator, he just kept stalking towards his car, passing a sedan, then a VW bus. That this course would walk him past the man in the blue suit was unavoidable, but in thirty seconds he could be behind the Nissan's wheel and speeding away to Kimmie's.

"It is Mr. Sorley, isn't it?" the man asked again. Rain was trying to give him a wide berth, but the man in the suit wasn't having it. "You fit the general description."

*Don't engage. Don't engage. Don't engage.* Rain kept his head down and his feet pumping, passing a coupe, an old Corvette, a van. Now the man in the suit was following him, walking briskly backwards without much effort. "There was an incident in this parking garage a couple of weeks ago. I understand you were a witness."

The strange waved his badge at him again, a meaningless flick of the wrist. The smile painted across his face unnerved him as the man in the suit got to the Nissan first, leaning against the driver's side door. "I'm sorry to disturb you, but do you have time for a few questions?"

"Get off my car." Rain tried to growl it, but it came out like a cough.

The man in the suit raised an eyebrow. "No."

"If you're a cop—" For some reason the *if* had just dropped in there, and that subconscious thought worried Rain more than any other. That the man's smile widened didn't help. "—If you're a cop, you can't just keep me here."

The man in the suit spread his hands wide. "Go wherever you like, Mr. Sorley. I'm just standing in the parking garage."

"Let me see your badge."

"You've already seen it."

"Flopping it around doesn't count."

The man smiled again and opened the leather case. "Are you going to authenticate it? You're some kind of badge expert who studies police identification in his spare time? Can tell a harbor patrolman from TSA at twenty paces, right?"

Rain studied the case. Yep, there was an ID, and there was a badge. This wasn't the *ah-ha* moment he had foreseen.

Exasperated, he tried again. "What do you want?"

"To ask you a few questions. Were you aware that there was an assault in this garage a couple weeks ago?"

"No." He had nothing to gain by cooperating, and thoughts of Kimmie wearing minimal clothing made him want to get out of there as fast as possible.

"Really?" The man in the suit looked like he was trying to shrug, but didn't have the body to accomplish it. "Got a nasty little cut on your scalp there. Where'd that come from?"

"My dog. Scratched me in my sleep."

The stranger tutted. "Don't lie to an officer, kid. We've got a witness that puts you at the scene."

"Kind of impossible, since I wasn't there. Are you done?"

"I'm just getting warmed up. This your car?"

The uncomfortable feeling intensified, and Rain leaned against the trunk of the car. Another glance told him no one was behind him, but he couldn't shake the feeling that someone else was in the shadows, watching. "Yeah. It's mine. Get off it."

"Do you want to talk about what happened to your assailant?"

"I told you, I don't know—"

"Cut the shit, kid. It's insulting. Do you think I just picked you at random? Do you think I just lurked in this cold fucking parking garage all day and chased poor bastards stepping off the elevator?"

"I—"

"Some shithead mugger jumped you, beat your ass. Until all of a sudden he couldn't. Do you want to talk about what you did to him?"

"That didn't—"

"We have surveillance tapes. We know all about it." The man in the suit reached into his jacket.

Rain paused, his brow furrowing, and looked around. "There aren't any cameras down here."

The man in the suit nodded and drew his pistol. It looked like the embodiment of night. "Then you see your predicament, right?"

"What?"

"Get in the van." The man in the suit motioned past Rain. There was indeed a van, black and windowless, eight cars up. "I'm not going to repeat myself."

For some reason, the gun wasn't completely freaking Rain out this time. Maybe he was getting used to them. "Wait. Who the fuck are you?"

"What does it matter?" The man in the suit took a menacing step towards him, raising the pistol to eye level. The barrel became the size of a well. "I'm the guy with the gun. The van."

Rain took a step backward, and then another. "Hold on. You're not going to just shoot me."

"Aren't I?"

"You need me for something."

"What? Now you want to talk about the mugging?"

A strange sensation was building, as if everything below his skin was beginning to catch fire. On its heels, he realized the dumpling incident had been no nightmare. Just Rain, and what he could do. "Who do you work for?"

"The Bay City Rollers. Get in the fucking van, kid."

"I'm not going anywhere with you." His fingertips itched as if a phoenix was just below his skin.

"Look, I don't think you understand the situation. I have a gun. Ergo, I make the rules. *Vae victus.*" He ran his free hand over his balding pate and pushed forward, trying to drive Rain towards the van. "I'll shoot you in the leg. Then the other leg, because if I have to shoot you once it's really no effort to do it again. The gunshots will be loud, and they might attract attention, even in this dump, so we'll have to leave very quickly. If I have to do that, I'll find a nice quiet rest stop by the river, pull over, and I'll do you some real damage before we get where we're going. I'm not a pro, but I make up for it with my enthusiasm. When I'm done, two bullets in your knees would feel like Farah Fawcett's blowing you. I—"

Rain batted aside the outstretched pistol and wrapped his palm across the stranger's face. The man in the suit fired. The roar was deafening against the concrete.

Then the fire flooded from Rain's fingertips, and the man screamed.

Only once. It was all he had time for.

Rain was operating on pure instinct. A great rush of heat, and then the man in the suit's face buckled inward. Bone became cartilage, became tissue. The man's skull liquefied, the spine following suit. Without support or structure, under the weight of his own flesh the man collapsed, discernible features congealing and spilling downward as from a broken bottle of ketchup.

Skin hung from Rain's fingers like a bloody pelt as the man in the suit bonelessly splashed onto the floor in wet rivulets, puddling beneath his clothing in a pinkish-red mess. The flood slopped around Rain's feet as it followed the angle of the concrete floor, an obscene oil slick seeping down the drive to find the lowest point.

He stared at his work in mute horror. The neat blue suit floated away with the tide.


He sat in the Nissan outside Kimmie's apartment for at least fifteen minutes, head pressed against the wheel, trying to pull it together. He was failing. After the human soup had simply dripped away down the ramp to the lowest levels of the garage, he'd broken the window of the black van and rifled through the glove compartment. There was nothing in there, not even the registration. Whoever he'd just turned into broth had been a ghost.

Twice in two weeks he'd had a gun pulled on him in the hospital garage. It couldn't be a coincidence. What the hell was happening? Who had the man been? Worst of all, where could he park?

Rain's shoes were a complete loss, abattoir chic, and he'd thrown them in a trash bin off of Killingsworth and 38th. He'd had an old pair of sneakers in his trunk for his infrequent visits to the gym, and he'd slipped these on with a thousand-mile-stare. The pants had been salvageable, and somehow he'd melted a man without getting any blood on his shirt.

*There never was a nightmare. You had to hose him off your feet.*

All of that, though, had not dissuaded him from going over to Kimmie's. Maybe it was pathetic, maybe it was some life-in-the-middle-of-so-much-death bullshit, but he still wanted her. He wasn't the most socially attuned, but if he called their rendezvous off, he thought the chances were pretty good she'd drop him like a dead spider.

After checking the rearview mirror to see how haunted his eyes were (verdict: somewhere below traipsing through a mine field, somewhere above gory-accident witness), he'd gone up to her door and knocked. If this went badly, he'd always have the picture messages.

She'd greeted him in a t-shirt and jeans, ushering him inside. In the back of his mind he'd been hoping for whipped cream, but what the hell.

Kimmie got him a beer from the fridge, which he accepted gratefully after semi-collapsing on her couch. He didn't recognize the brand, but the cold hoppy mess was amazing. He wondered if he was developing a taste for pine tar.

The apartment was nice, if a little white and vacant. There wasn't much in the way of decoration aside from a few keepsakes and framed pictures, mostly of Kimmie and friends. Her shelves consisted mostly of popular blu-rays and the occasional self-help book. It reminded him a little of an IKEA staging.

She made herself a drink, something pink with clinking ice, and sat down onto the couch next to him. He didn't think it was her first of the night.

Kimmie was stunning, almost a carnal totem. Her shiny brown hair bounced around her shoulders like a shampoo commercial, and her wide blue eyes and open manicured gestures made everything she said seem of wide and cosmic importance. As Rain was having a hard time not flashing back at the moment to creating a human grease trap or picturing the two of them deep in sexual overtures, he was probably missing a good deal of her actual words but thought he was attuned to the overall context.

Letting him know that she was usually not this kind of girl was first, but she thought they really had this kind of connection, you know? Rain nodded along dutifully, remembering the squelching sounds and red footprints his ruined shoes had made as he'd run back to the Nissan. Tilting the bottle back, he found that his beer was empty and Kimmie got him another one, this time positioning herself slightly closer to him on the couch.

She told him a little about herself, growing up poor in a little town outside of Missing Mile, North Carolina. How she'd run away from an abusive father who'd broken her arm at fourteen, taking a midnight bus ride as far as Oklahoma, then hitching the rest of the way to San Francisco, which had involved at least a couple of hair-raising adventures and one midnight fight in a graveyard. She'd waited tables under a different name for a while before getting involved in modeling, then dancing, and then exotically dancing her way through a business degree. She'd just been getting her company off the ground before the tech boom had driven rents through the roof and pushed her out, and she'd landed here.

He appreciated her openness. He also appreciated that he was almost certainly a murderer, with bloody hands that would never quite come clean. Kimmie went to the kitchen, refreshed her drink, and brought him back another beer.

Kimmie told him that the night before had been incredible, and his attention started to focus. When she said she'd never experienced anything quite like it, Rain felt heat begin to suffuse his cheeks as his blood pressure dropped. She put her hand on his knee, and he thought of the detective's hand dissolving like a rubber glove filled with gravy. Kimmie asked if he was okay, maybe a little distracted?

He didn't mention either his aunt or slaying a man in a parking garage, but chalked it up to having a lot on his mind. *More mystery, less history,* Ronnie would have said.

He had no idea how well this was or was not going until Kimmie set her drink down, tearing off her t-shirt and straddling him. At that point he felt he was doing okay. Her exquisite breasts were inches from his face, a solidity stirring in his jeans, when something she said finally caused him to snap out of it.

"—I know what you can do."

Not entirely sure, he pushed aside an image of a man melting like candle wax and tried to jump in. "Yeah? What do you want me to do?"

She put her hands on his shoulders and pushed him

back, her chest bobbing with the effort. It was making conversation difficult. "Do you want a list?"

He nodded, figuring that it would at the least play into his fantasies for the next week or so. Come to think of it, this whole thing seemed too good to be true.

She smiled. "I said I know what you can do. That you can change the way you look." Kimmie paused with tentative determination. "I want you to change me too."

Rain's mind attempted to snap to attention, but the increasing pressure at his groin was making it no easy feat. Still, he struggled from imminent pleasure to form a coherent thought. It wasn't the greatest intellectual parry, but it was all he could manage. "What?"

"Last night. You kept getting bigger, and then I swear your face changed."

He tried again. "What?"

She smiled, hair fluttering around her face, and leaned closer. Her chest pressed warmly against his. "You were in my mouth, a little average but doing all right, and I told you that you were big, how I loved how big you were. I mean, I'm paraphrasing, but you get the drift. You pulled my hair a little and then suddenly you swelled, got bigger, like inhumanly. I've had some guys in my mouth before, and trust me. That shit is not natural."

Her tongue flicked out and found his ear. "Then I made eye contact. You loved it, but then your face became more— I don't know how to describe it. Defined. Chiseled. And then—well, you know what happened."

She ground herself against him, which really wasn't helping his coherent thoughts flow, but he tried anyway. "No—"

"I know what I saw. What I felt." She licked her lips at the last, a flicker of tongue, and Rain wondered with startling clarity if this was all a show for his benefit. "You can change the way you look. Make things bigger, or smaller?

Can you change other people?"

She inched up and put her chest closer to his face. Rain, who had never been a good liar under the best of circumstances, failed again. "I don't think so."

"Really?" Kimmie pulled back a little. "Have you ever tried?"

Rain was mute, settling instead for wrapping his hands around her hips. She laughed. "Is that a yes?"

He didn't really want to think about Ronnie's junk right now or puddles of man, so he pulled her tighter against him. She laughed and put a hand on his chest. "Slow down, cowboy. I want an answer."

"Once." He reconsidered. "Kind of twice."

"Did it work?" She slipped her fingers lower, tracing the bulge in his jeans.

Rain groaned, not sure if it was worse to find himself in this situation or that his libido was refusing to extract him from it. "Yeah."

"Can you do me?" She pressed down a little harder, and he gasped.

The obvious answer came and went. "You're beautiful."

Kimmie laughed. It was not beautiful. "Flattery only takes you so far. I'm maybe a Portland 9. There are things I'd change if I could. If *you* could."

She readjusted, lifting her hips and sliding her hand beneath the waistband of his jeans. "We could be really good together, you and I. It's just a little thing."

His breath was coming in hard fits. "What do you want me to do?"

Kimmie grinned. Her fingers found him and squeezed. "Look under my eyes."

They were a little wild. "Okay."

"See the wrinkles? The little crow's feet? The start of circles underneath?" Rain had to allow that he couldn't, but she shook her head. "You've already fucked me. You don't need to play nice right now. I want them smoothed out. I want them gone."

Her hand sped up. "Do it for me, Hank. And I'll do something amazing for you."

Rain found his hands raising to her before it came to him. *Wait. Did she just forget who I was, or did I give her a fake name last night?*

Already not thinking clearly, he pushed that thought aside for later. "You've got to hold still a little."

"Do you *really* want me to hold still?"

"Your head, at least." He cradled her face, thumbs tracing lightly beneath her eyelashes. He was aware of the ripsawing motion of her forearm, the inevitable building within him, but Rain tried to concentrate, let the feeling pour through him while simultaneously not letting the other rip him apart.

This was simple. Just smoothing something down. If he could reconstruct Ronnie—

—*image leave my head*—

—this should be child's play.

She squeezed him harder, and he gasped. "Come on, cowboy."

The burning sensation began in his forearms and traced its way to his fingertips, painful but also this time spiked with pleasure. The myriad of sensations was almost too much to bear, and he moaned as the power flowed into her.

She grunted, the minute agony of reconstruction hitting her. And then everything went very wrong.

Rain pressed lightly with his thumbs. For a moment he thought it was working, but then his thumbs sunk into her eye sockets like crimson putty. Instead of smoothing the skin of her cheeks, the red cords of muscle now clung to him like bloody taffy. They stretched and pulled, his fingers wrenching bowstrings of sinew and muscle outwards in a marionette horror.

Kimmie screamed. For some reason her hand continued to work at him, but any erection he may have had was suddenly gone, and she ground his flaccid cock unmercifully. Her eyes were open, and she spit out words like a mantra.

"—what the fuck what the fuck what the fuck—"

He tried to put the gobbets back, restore them, but his fingers only plunged deeper. She howled as her forehead drooped, then sloughed downward.

Rain panicked, unable to abort the mission but just as clueless as to how to save it. He tried pulling himself back, the burning in his wrists now a raging immolation. Kimmie's features began to buckle, to run. A solid wave of flesh puddled downwards, burying her eyes, covering her mouth. By some small miracle her nostrils remained intact.

Finally freeing himself, he yanked his hands away. The molding had been a success.

The circles under her eyes were smooth and flawless. So was the rest of her face, a flesh pink moon without feature.

She was making a sound, a horrible, muffled caw. It took Rain a second to realize that it was what screaming sounded like without a mouth.

Kimmie lurched to her feet, breasts bouncing, fingers clawing at the flat plane of her face. She twisted and bolted for the kitchen, flailing arms sending bric-a-brac flying. Colliding with the counter, she rebounded, sending the vodka bottle crashing to the tile before knocking over two cute barstools and plunging towards the dinette. That awful muted howl kept pouring from her somehow as she hit the little table, slid off it, and caromed towards Rain. He screamed at her to stop.

Her knees slammed into the coffee table, and she went sprawling. With a dull *thud* her forehead bounced off the arm of the couch, and she slumped motionless to the carpet.

Rain leapt to his feet, his mind now a completely blank canvas. A hundred feats and actions played out in his mind. He made none of them.

Kimmie stayed down, her beautiful hair shadowing her face like an auburn mask. His hand found the bottle of beer unbidden and brought it to his lips. It disappeared with three gasping gulps.

Rain didn't say her name, only knelt down to check. She was breathing.

He could fix this.

Could he fix this?

Wavering white stars danced on the outskirts of his vision. His fingers had gone completely numb.

His heart thrummed in his chest, his breathing ragged. The room began to spin, just a little.

*Get a fucking grip on yourself. You're not the victim here.*

Panting, he willed himself to take slow, deep breaths. He rolled her over onto her back.

Kimmie's face resembled nothing so much as a pink hard-boiled egg. She wasn't moving.

Taking a deep breath, he tried to recall all the sculpting how-to's he'd watched on the internet over the last couple of weeks. He studied her for a moment, retrieving her t-shirt and draping it over her chest, still distracted. With a burst of inspiration, he dug his phone out of his pocket, scrolling through the messages she'd sent him.

He tried to create a composite of her face in his mind's eye, taking each image in turn and transposing it onto the whole. He could do this.

Oh, he didn't know if he could do this.

Reaching down, he placed his fingers on either side of her skull.

Nothing happened.

Rain shook his hands like an accomplished mime, willing the feeling back into them, hoping for the familiar fire. He rested them back onto her smooth, horrible face.

Nothing happened.


Over the next fifteen minutes, he helped himself to another two beers, put his head in his hands, and felt really sorry for himself.

Rain couldn't help it. He knew it was grotesque, that he wasn't the one whose face looked like the empty page in a police sketchbook, but still.

He'd finally found someone, someone who seemed genuinely interested in him. That she was a knockout to boot was only gummy bears on the sundae of romance, but it had only taken him twenty-four hours to ruin it, irreversibly maim her, and wonder if he should start wiping the apartment clean of his DNA. Standing outside of her window with a boom-box was not going to cut it.

The problem was, he thought, that he had no idea what the limits of this power were. The most he'd molded in a day before had been turning his assailant into a fucked-up beholder. Today he had improved Ronnie's love life, transformed someone into liquid gore, and now this.

Wandering about the apartment in a near panic, he'd looked in the mirror. Something about his appearance was perceptibly different, a noticeable improvement even though he hadn't so much as touched his face since the first night. He had a second to wonder if his subconscious was rewriting him on the sly. Was it some outer transformation to match how he felt on the inside?

If so, he was about to get real ugly.

Kneading his temples, he wandered back to the kitchen, got another beer, and returned to the couch. Shaking his wrists like he had a terminal case of jazz hands, he tried to concentrate. All he needed was enough juice for one more fix, and then he could put it up for a while.

It was then he realized that Kimmie was gone.

There was only one bedroom. Rain instead gave the bathroom a once-over and searched the tub. When he came back out onto the short corridor, he heard a shunted wheezing coming from the next room.

Her bedroom was dark. Rain fumbled for the switch but couldn't find it, and instead just followed the muffled whimpers. From the door-length mirror on the closet, he could see her wedged between the bed and the nightstand, a robe draped around her shoulders, head down. It took him a moment to realize that she was sobbing.

"Hey," he said. If there was a prize for least-comforting understatement, it was already in the mail, but words like so much else were failing him. "Hey."

She turned towards the sound of his voice, the flattened plane of her face gleaming in the light from the hallway. Kimmie made a sound that could have been anything.

"Don't worry," he said. His heart ached. If he could have just been himself, just shown her who he really was—

*—she never would have spoken to you in the first place—*

—and kept this flesh molding thing out of it, none of this would have happened. She wouldn't be blind and mute, cowering in the corner.

He was the lowest of the low. Rain circled the bed and put a hand on her shoulder. Kimmie jerked away with a grunt.

"Shh," he said before realizing that she couldn't yell even if she wanted to. "I've got this. I'm going to fix it."

He rested his hands across her perfect cheekbones. This time, she didn't pull away.

Rain pictured her composite, all the photos she had sent blurring together into a single primal mold. Breathing slowed down, time fell away, and in that moment he was a sculptor presented with new clay.

His fingers caught fire and danced.

This time it really hurt him, a bone-grating shred from his wrists to his shoulders that reverberated all the way down his spine. But her cheeks gained definition, her forehead restoring itself. Her lips emerged, gained definition, and those green eyes freed themselves from the flood. The relief in them was unmistakable.

It took less than three minutes before he had to fall away, blood thundering in his chest. It felt like he'd run a marathon chained to a battleship. Kimmie pushed him down and ran to the bathroom.

She was gone for what seemed like an absurdly long amount of time. Then again, he hadn't been the one transformed into a tabula rasa, so he crept back to the kitchen and helped himself to another beer.

There was really something to this pine tar.

Finally she came out into the living room. In the heat of the moment, he hadn't really studied the finished product, but he had to admit that she looked stunning.

Kimmie regarded him coolly on the couch. She made no move to join him. "Is it always like that when you do other people?" she asked.

"Yeah," he lied. It came out smoothly and without provocation.

She nodded and said nothing, a war of emotions firing cannons behind her eyes. "Probably should have given me a heads-up, then."

"Yeah."

"Well, it worked." Kimmie leaned in closer to him and tilted her head to catch the light. Beneath her eyes the skin shone, smooth and flawless.

"Cool."

She sighed. "I'm going to need you to get the fuck out."


His cubicle was shrinking.

It was all he could think of that morning. Not the night before, not being exorcised from Kimmie's life, not the numbers he could make dance around the screen in little columns and rows. Rain was convinced that the barriers had shrunk by at least three inches, and now he could barely get his elbows up without smacking them against the walls.

Pulling his phone out, he checked it for the twentieth time that day. No messages, no calls. Rain wasn't surprised that his fling with Kimmie had flamed out, but to do it in such a grand five-alarm fashion had really sent the message that he was going to die alone.

With this and other cheerful ponderings, he pored through his work pipeline with the unremitting focus of someone who really, really doesn't want to think about anything else. It was almost time for lunch before he noticed Ronnie hovering around his periphery like a float in a white dress shirt.

"Ronnie?"

"Hey, Wolfcastle." The big man greeted him with the amount of enthusiasm usually reserved for deadbeat dads and serial killers. "Listen, do you want to grab lunch in a little bit? I'm buying."

This stunned Rain into silence, which was good as Ronnie had no intention of letting him speak. "The new plumbing's working good as advertised, but remember that second favor? I want to talk to you about that."

"Okay. Lunch then." Rain nodded. He was numb and tired and not in the mood at all, but it wasn't as if he had a surplus of friends making demands on his time.

And free food was free food.

It took him most of the next hour to finish up the morning pipeline. He cleared out and wandered by Ronnie's workspace only to find it empty. Strange, but it looked like Ronnie's cubicle was shrinking too.

He found the big man in the lunch room, his narrow table shoved against the far wall. Ronnie motioned him to sit and slid a twelve-inch hoagie wrapped in yellow paper across the checkered surface.

Unwrapping the package, Rain let out a whistle. "You sprang for fries too? Seriously, Ronnie, are you dying?"

"You know that's not funny," the big man said. "Look, I wanted to run something by you. I'm not sure if you can help me out, but I thought I'd try, you know?"

Rain hadn't realized how hungry he was. Around

mouthfuls of sandwich he managed to growl his agreement.

Ronnie sighed. "Here's the thing. I may not have been completely, completely honest with you the other night. I'm a big guy, and even with a big hog, I'm not doing so well."

"Uh-huh."

"Now I've got more confidence, but still. I don't *feel* it. I'm a three hundred pound bull smashing through the bottle shop. If I'd kept in shape after football, eaten right, worked out—" Ronnie sighed. "People are going to be into me. Nature of the beast. But I want to widen that demographic."

The first warning bells began to ring in Rain's skull. He tried to still them with more sandwich.

"I was watching *Conan* last night. Not the one with the white governor, but with that hunk of burnin' Hawaiian. And I thought, that guy is built like me."

Neither able to confirm or deny, Rain kept eating. "Uh-huh."

"You get it. I mean, sure, I've got the bulk, but underneath all of it is a muscle-ripped man machine. That's never gone away. A little spit and polish, and I could be back in that kind of shape. I'd be back to twenty-five percent or better, getting all kinds of honeys. Just slaying them at the club."

*Or in the parking garage.* Rain was depressed to find that he was almost out of sandwich. "So you've decided to exercise and eat right?"

Ronnie raised an eyebrow. "Really, amigo?"

A sinking feeling in his stomach threatened his sandwich to come up. *Here we go.* "Look, Ronnie, this— this thing. There's been some really weird side effects lately."

"Yeah? The only one I've seen is bringing home bombshells from the bar." The big man folded his massive arms across his chest. "So that's how it is, then? You owe me a favor, but you're going to hold out on me."

"Ronnie—"

"No, no, no. I see how it is. Listen, *mijo*, it's going to take years to get back into that kind of shape, during which

I could have a heart attack on the fucking Stairmaster. You can make it happen *tonight*."

"I melted someone's face off last night."

This seemed to give Ronnie pause. "But they're okay now, right?"

"Not talking to me, but yeah."

"Well, okay then." The big man leaned across the table. "You've been given a gift. What better use for it than to help your friends? And, bonus, we'll be square after this. No more favors."

"I've never taken—stuff—out of someone before. Just moved it around."

"Yeah?" Ronnie nodded and took a bite of his sandwich coolly.

"Well, the obvious question is where to put it."

"Flush it down the toilet. Fill the trash can by the sink. I'm not sentimental."

The warning bells had risen to an air-raid siren, but Rain was choosing to ignore them. Maybe he could put the molding away for a while. Drive it underground before things got any crazier. Only two people knew at this point, and one of them was conveniently not speaking to him. If he could get the other one off his back, he'd be home free.

"Okay. Just say when."


The dingy bathroom was hotter than it needed to be, and every breath he took tasted stale. Rain wondered if EpiCo had limited the air conditioning on the closed floor to cut costs, especially since they were now after hours. With no idea how long this might take, he didn't want his manager coming downstairs to look for him if he ran over his fifteen minute break, so they'd waited until after five to make the impromptu surgery happen. The yellow light leaking through the walls of the big stall was somehow ominous, foreboding, and part of him had no interest in going through with it. The other—

It was a tool, he thought. Like all tools, it wanted to be used. Rain had to admit that he didn't know the boundaries yet, or what his limits were, but a small part of him was aching to find out.

Besides, he'd be free of obligation soon. With Ronnie's silence bought and Kimmie's forced, he'd owe no more favors, no more molding. If he wanted, maybe he could be done with it for a while.

The wet patch above him appeared to have spread. Rain retraced the office layout in his mind, trying to figure out what was directly over the stall on the third floor. The copier? One of the tech support desks? The break room fridge?

He heard the restroom door creak open and heavy footfalls traipse across the tiles. Three knocks, and Ronnie barged in. "You ready to go, amigo?"

Rain was, in fact, ready to go. He'd hauled in the trash can by the sink and another two smaller ones he'd found in a second- floor storage closet, and right now just wanted nothing more than to get this over with. "Yeah."

The big man slipped inside the stall. His eyes were wide and jittery, the extra bounce in his step like a child's on Christmas. "All right. Let's do this!"

"Yeah. Um, I've been trying to figure out the logistics of—whatever this is all afternoon." He tried to think of a delicate way to put this. "You should probably strip."

"Ah-cha-cha!" Ronnie began to gyrate as he unbuttoned his shirt. Rain forced himself to relax.

"Okay. As a reminder, I'm pretty sure I can do this, but—" Rain would have a chance to think on the next sentence in the following days and wonder as to his gift for precognitive understatement. "Things could get messy."

"When don't they?" Ronnie shimmied out of his pants gracefully and hung them on the hook on the bottom of the door. Maybe this could all work out, Rain thought.

"I'm going to sculpt you to where you want to be, then

59

drain the excess completely out of you. That's the plan?"

"The plan." Ronnie held up a still image from *Conan* on his phone. "Like that. Only more manly."

"Huh." Rain shook his head, rubbing his palms together. The sheer bulk of the big man and the trash can were already making the stall pretty cramped. At least there was plenty to work with. "Remember, I've never done this before."

"Don't worry, mijo." The big man clapped his shoulder. "I believe in you."

"Are you ready?"

"Born that way, amigo. Just remember: leave my dick alone."

With a deep breath, Rain raised his hands. Something like fire jumped between them.

He settled his palms on Ronnie's belly and concentrated. A picture formed in his mind's eye, Conan from the phone battling tentacled monstrosities, sword glinting, muscles rippling, and then he slowly removed the steel and monster from the equation. The burning sensation rose to his fingertips, a white-hot sun held between his hands.

The pain was immense, a ligament-shredding agony that dropped Rain to one knee. Ronnie grunted, his eyes rolling back. "*Fuck fuck fuck—*" he began to moan, but then even the profanity became too much for him.

Beneath his skin, muscle and sinew moved and shifted, tectonic plates forming a new Pangea. The shelf of the big man's chest rose and hardened. His shoulders expanded, deltoids rising from lost tendrils to his thickening neck. Thighs coalesced into barrels, calves ballooning.

The suffering plateaued in waves. It wasn't so much as that it stopped as that he had found the reins and could ride it for a while before it bucked him off again. Truth be told, beneath it there was almost pleasure. Here he was, a sculptor with a hunk of clay, able to mold and shape it into whatever suited his fancy. Creation bled from his fingertips. He felt like an artist. He felt like a god.

Ronnie drew sharp, panting breaths, sweat pouring down his forehead. Forearms swelled, veins like steel cables rising to the surface. Biceps plumped outward like hams. The big man's jowls retreated, jaw gaining definition and shadow. Rain made and made and made.

And then he was finished sculpting, and it was time to take out the trash.

He cupped his hands together, fingers forming a bowl, and pressed it into Ronnie's gut. The big man howled as his digits sunk in, beneath the epidermis, then the subcutaneous fat, and finally deep below the muscle. He penetrated Ronnie up to his wrists and sighed, the pyretic fury boiling from his palms, and then pulled.

Rain wasn't ready for what happened next. A looping coil of white and red glistening flesh leapt out from the hole he'd made, illogically shooting upwards to stretch almost to the ceiling. It reminded Rain of an antique photograph he'd seen once of a seance, the medium coughing out a cloud of ectoplasm. The marbled material hung in the air, a hose spooling into a shapeless pile.

More and more flooded to the ceiling as the big man lessened. The mass was the size of a cat now, then a beagle, a cloud of amorphous gore that grew thunderheads and rose. Rain felt like a magician pulling endless scarves from his hat, yanking out knot after knot with no end in sight. He tried to direct the shape to the trash can, cognizant that gravity at some point was going to reassert itself and cover the both of them in human tallow, but somehow could not get it to move.

Ronnie screamed, a surprisingly high yelp that echoed off the tiles. Wasting away, he stepped back, knee connecting with the toilet, and toppled to the floor as the floating grotesquerie gained the size of a collie.

Joined by the wrists, Rain plummeted with him, head cracking against the porcelain rim. White stars danced around him, and one eye quickly filmed over with red. He couldn't break the connection, but his scalp was sticky with blood.

The thing was as big as a goat now, roiling and formless. Rain surveyed his handiwork, vision half clear and half crimson. Ronnie had leaned out, bodybuilder muscle now standing in stark relief against his skin. The time had come to pull the plug.

Drawing his hands back slowly, Rain closed his palms together, severing the tie. The last coil whipped into the beefy mass by the ceiling and quivered there expectantly.

Rain withdrew his fingers, closing the hole he'd left in the big man's abdomen. Ronnie's eyes rolled back to the whites, a litany of profanity dripping from his lips that did not stop as Rain slumped against the stall door, heart pounding, breath impossible to catch.

Absently Rain ran his hands along his scalp and found the ragged edges of the wound, melding them together without a second thought. He tried to rub the blood out of his eye and watched Ronnie stumble to his feet, stretching out his arms before turning in a pirouette. "Dude, that really fucking hurt."

"Yeah?" Rain's fingers were numb. Every breath he took seemed to rattle in his lungs. "No shit?"

"No shit." Ronnie flexed a bicep, then both at the same time. He looked down at his stomach with something like wonder, hands dancing across the sculpted muscle of his abdomen. "Holy shit, amigo, but you really came through."

"Yeah." Rain was seeing everything in a kind of bloody 3-D. There was one golden Ronnie, one scarlet one, the images superimposing. He was entirely new, a behemoth of polished muscle. Rain could hardly believe it himself.

Ronnie squatted, pivoted, got up on his toes. "This is incredible, amigo. This is crazy." He glanced up at the ceiling, at the gory bulk of his extract, and extended a finger. "What are you going to with that?"

None of them could have been prepared for what happened next. It was the kind of situation that really just fell outside the extent of human experience, and in the days that followed Rain tried to remind himself that he was almost guiltless. He *had* never done this before. Out of all the possible outcomes, who could have foreseen it?

The amorphous mass began to pucker and retreat. A divot formed at its fore and sunk inwards towards the core.

"What's it doing?" Ronnie asked.

All at once the gory blob of tissue poured from the ceiling to the ground. The sound it made was a side of beef getting creamed by a truck.

Before they could react, it surged up from the tiles. Rain saw it raise itself as two beefy legs took shape, two fleshy stalks extending from its core, a puppet being made from bloody hamburger.

It then launched itself at Ronnie. An oval shape like a head rose from what would have been the torso as the boneless thing rammed into the big man.

Maybe the size of an eight-year-old, it had assumed the shape of its former host. And it was pissed.

The thing threw a series of wet punches at Ronnie that probably would have been harmless had he not been so utterly dumbstruck at what was happening. They left bloody spatters on his stomach as the big man reeled backwards into the trash cans, sending them both toppling to the floor.

The meat puppet leapt onto Ronnie's chest. Things that were not quite hands were forming at the ends of its boneless appendages, and it thrust these down at his throat, wrapping them around the big man's windpipe and squeezing.

Rain thought he had lost his mind. That was the only possible explanation for what he was seeing, this grotesque silhouette astride his friend, armstalks crushing his neck. All of it felt like just a lucid dream, floating on the edges of reality.

The big man gargled, spat, and wheezed. It was decidedly undreamlike.

*Shit.* He struggled to his feet, grabbed the puppet where

the shoulders might have been, and tried to pull the thing off of Ronnie.

It snapped its head around and hissed at him. The move was so startling that he backed away for a second.

*It has no mouth. How the hell can it hiss?*

Ronnie was turning an alarming shade of purple on the floor, his shoes spanking frantically against the cheap tile. He was trying to push the meat puppet aside, but his hands couldn't find any purchase. Each shove simply sunk into and through the thing's flabby core, again and again. Eyeless, it stared down at him balefully as his struggles began to fade.

Rain did the only thing he could think of. He stepped forward and kicked through the meat puppet's armstalks, meaning to batter them aside. Instead his foot passed completely through them in a bloody cloud of torn flesh. The hand-like growths fell and flopped in wet splashes against the floor.

The thing growled at him again as Ronnie took a gasping inhalation, then another. His chest had been stained red with puppet juice.

Scampering away, the homunculus bent down, levering out its stumps. The growths flowed upwards into the meat puppet's core as new, more realized shapes sprung from its arms.

The thing lowered them to Ronnie's throat again. Not even thinking, Rain felt the burning sensation in his hands trigger and ignite as he grabbed the meat puppet and hurled it against the wall.

It struck the tile with a horrible wet spattering sound, and then the thing staggered to what may have been its feet. Faceless and ill-proportioned, it was a golem made of ground beef, but the round ball on its shoulders gave him a look that could only be wounded betrayal.

*Holy shit, does this thing have feelings?*

The meat puppet bolted past him, leaving a red smear against the wall as it threw open the door to the stall and ran out into the bathroom. He tried to chase after it and slipped in a puddle of blood and grease. For the second time in five minutes he found himself pratfalling to the hard tile. His hands barely got up to save himself a concussion against the toilet rim.

The bathroom door screeched open as the meat puppet wetly jogged outside. Rain tried to get up but slipped again. The squelching footsteps receded in the distance. Faintly, he thought he heard another door open and shut.

A hard iron ball formed in the pit of his stomach that only seemed to grow heavier. What the hell had he set loose in the world?

Ronnie sputtered and sat up, chest and arms covered in so much crimson that he looked like he'd been gored. He shook his head and gave Rain a lopsided grin. "Well, amigo. That seemed like a success."

# EPITHELIAL

Rain had followed the bloody footprints, suddenly very conscious of his fragile employment.

They led him on a merry sprint down the hall. Dark red smears on doorknobs glistened where it had tried and failed to find an exit before it eventually had chanced onto the stairwell. From there the stains took him downward, all the way to the first floor and out the side exit. Gory not-quite-handprints on the door told him all he needed to know.

Outside the tracks disappeared onto the small manicured lawn, and the trail ran cold. Of the meat puppet, there was no sign.

Rain expected to hear screams of terror, the squeal of brakes, the blaring of car horns. Instead he was treated to the placid hum of a normal Tuesday night.

*Will it keep living indefinitely? It can't just go on, right?*

By the time he got back, Ronnie had paper toweled his demigod's physique off as best he could. His clothes sagged away from him now, and he had held his pants up with the air of a conquering hero as he thanked Rain before wandering down to his car.

His work had been impeccable, Rain had to admit. Knowing Ronnie, there had to be a way he'd fuck it all up.

Rain had cleaned up the rest of his impromptu surgery center as best he could. He was already late to see Aunt Lucy.

When he stepped out of the Nissan, there was a faint greasiness to the parking garage, a carnal stink just barely on the edge of his senses. The van was nowhere to be seen.

Rain stopped holding his breath only when he'd made it to the elevator and up to Room 38.

At last it was tranquil, and better yet silent. Aunt Lucy lay quietly beneath her blue sheets, no change perceptible in her condition. The whirring of the machines and the hiss of the respirator were now just background noise, an empty symphony that helped relax his fevered nerves. At some point he leaned back against the wall on the vinyl couch, put his head against the window, and closed his eyes.

"If I tell you visiting hours are over, are you going to roid rage on me?"

He startled, bouncing his head off of the windowpane. Masami laughed. "You look like some kind of rugged hell. Go home and get some sleep."

"Thanks," he murmured, shaking some of the cobwebs loose. He must have been out for an hour, maybe more. When was the last time he'd really slept?

Masami followed her usual routine, inspecting the patient and machines, making notes on some of the readouts. Rain watched her for a moment, a lean shadow slipping between the equipment. "How's she doing?"

"Fighting." Masami checked the plastic tubes jutting from the old woman's wrist. "She's tough. Tougher than I think I'd be, given the circumstances. But she won't wake up."

Rain felt a weight behind his lungs, his throat closing, and turned away. The nurse took his hand in hers. Her grip was surprisingly warm. "Hey. It's okay. She's doing the best she can. You've just got to make your peace with it."

Suddenly aware of their proximity, Rain pulled back a little. The feeling wasn't unpleasant, quite the opposite, but he currently had enough problems without crushing on the night nurse as well. "You're right."

She gave him a sad half-smile. "Yeah. I am. The hardest thing for us to accept is that there are times when we can't do anything."

Masami squeezed his hand and continued her patrol down the hallway. Rain watched her leave, the door swinging shut behind her, and looked at his aunt, lying there between the vinyl piping and machines.

The horrible thought was already taking shape.

*Can't I?*

Rain couldn't believe she'd called him back.

He'd checked his phone in the parking garage, suddenly conscious that it had been hours since he'd even thought about it. It wasn't as if he had a wide social circle that he was neglecting, or that Decker could call in complaints over his kibble quality, but like everyone else the device had burrowed into his routine. Neglect wasn't something that could go on indefinitely.

There were two texts and a voicemail. He was more than a little surprised to see who they were from.

Her voice was unnaturally cheery over the phone for an apology, professing that she'd overreacted and that she hoped he'd understand. Was he free tonight?

The two messages were only photos. If they were apologies, Rain was in for one hell of a night.

He wasn't sure what to make of it, only that he couldn't believe he was getting another chance with Kimmie. After all, there weren't many times that a prospective beau could melt someone's face off and still get a call back.

Rain's head ached and he was bone tired, but what else could he say? In moments like these he knew he was weak, a slave to the chemicals and hormones that whirled through his shivering flesh, but that didn't matter a bit.

He wanted more Kimmie. Needed it, in fact.

On the way out of the hospital garage, he could have sworn he saw the man in the blue suit again. Not exactly the same man, and then only for an instant before the headlights turned the corner and the shadows retook him, but Rain was almost positive. Panic filled his throat.

In a gutsy move, Rain hit the brakes and slammed the car into reverse, whipping his head around to double check. There was no one there.

Any eagerness quickly chilled before shattering. With a concrete wall behind him, there was nowhere the man could have gone. Was his conscience trying to haunt him, or had it just been a trick of the light?

*There couldn't be more than one, could there?*

When he got to her apartment, Kimmie answered her door *sans* whipped cream again. It was a flaw, but Rain was learning to live with it. "Thanks for coming."

"Thanks for having me." The apartment was spotless. Photos had been rehung, the shattered glass swept away. It was as if the night before had never happened. Rain hoped that it was a harbinger for their whole relationship.

She led him over to the couch and asked him if he wanted a beer. He thought some pine tar would go down great about now, and she got him one and made herself something dark and icy from the bottles on the counter. Rain admired her figure, the way her t-shirt clung to her, and for once tried to push everything else in his head aside.

"About last night—" she said, killing that idea.

"I'm sorry." It was out before he could even process the words.

Kimmie gave him an indecipherable look. "It was my fault. I put you up to it. I mean, you weren't ready. You even tried to warn me, but I didn't listen."

This didn't quite match Rain's memories, but since it

sounded like he was coming out ahead, he let it slide. "Okay."

She lowered herself to the couch, snuggling up to him. "Besides, the important part was that you were able to fix it in the end. No harm, no foul, right?"

"Yeah." And he had fixed it, hadn't he? Why would she still be upset?

*Because she was left blind with only two tiny holes to breathe through, Buffalo Bill. Get some perspective.*

That voice was really starting to kill the mood. Rain tried to squelch it.

"You have a gift," she continued. "I mean it. It's not fair for me to ask you to hide it, or smother it. You've got to let it blossom, you know?"

Rain didn't, but the warm press of her against him was once more making conscious thought a little difficult. "I think so."

"You have to touch me to make it happen, right? You can't just—I don't know, zap me from across the room?"

"Right," he tried.

"Oh, that's easy. All you have to do, then," she purred. "is refine your touch. And if there's one thing I can help you with, it's that."

His face flushed. The room seemed about twenty degrees hotter than it had before, and he took a swallow from the bottle rather than answer her. She didn't seem to notice.

"Can I ask you a question?" Kimmie finished her drink in a gulp, slammed the tumbler down on the coffee table, and slid her legs across his lap. Rain tried not to spit out his beer.

"Anything."

"If you could change one thing about me, what would it be?"

The gears turning in his head locked on emotional sediment and ground to a halt. There was no right answer to this, he thought, and cursed himself for sending that useful pragmatic voice away. "Nothing. I mean, you're gorgeous. You're you."

*Disaster averted.*

"No, I mean really. We've seen each other naked. None

of that cute shit." Kimmie turned her head this way and that, lifted her breasts in both hands and pushed them together. She stood up, pivoted, posed. "What would it be?"

Enjoying the display, Rain almost missed his cue. "Like I said, you're beautiful. I wouldn't change a thing."

Kimmie nodded, as if she knew that this would take some patience. "Do you know what I would change?"

Rain couldn't believe it.

She'd gone down on him first after he'd tweaked her nose, just a tiny bit. In a way, he'd proved her completely right. Everything was just a matter of touch, and instead of going at the clay with a hammer and chisel and just hoping for the best, he could simply use a delicate file to sand some fine edges away.

Had her breasts been perfect? Not according to her. When she'd finished with him the first time, she'd slipped his hands beneath her shirt to help change his mind. He'd been all too willing to help her see her perfection, after which she'd returned the favor.

Rain had never been a repeat performer before. It hadn't ever seemed remotely possible, and now that it was, the two of them went on like that for quite a while. A tuck to the waist here, a smoothing of wrinkles there, punctuated with hearty sex until he felt dehydrated and seriously on the verge of collapse.

She was his goddess. He wanted her to see herself the way he saw her. It was as simple as that, and that she kept balling him after every modification was just icing on the cake.

She showed him the door somewhere around two in the morning. With a kiss goodnight and a flick to his already responding junk, Kimmie had shut the door.

Over the next few days, Rain established something of a routine. He'd go to work, come home to feed Decker, visit his aunt, and then over to Kimmie's for a night of wild sex and body molding before slinking out at two in the morning, crashing at his apartment, and starting the whole process back up again in four hours.

It was exhausting, but she was insatiable.

They never left her apartment. They never stopped. As soon as he entered her apartment, their clothes were off and they were going at it like lemurs on ecstasy.

Rain had never felt this way before. What he was feeling exactly was mostly a mixture of exhaustion, soreness, and afterglow, but it was certainly novel. The modifications now had become small, little touches here carefully applied. Kimmie studied herself in the door-length mirror of her closet with surgical appraisal, always asking Rain's opinion about the shape of this, the curve of that. He was more than happy to oblige her, then, any way he could. The goddess had even admitted that she was *so close* to perfection, if not for a blemish on her calf, a slight asymmetry to her backside.

The final list kept changing, but that was fine. All he wanted was to make her happy, to find herself beautiful and perfect. And it helped that the sex was mind-blowing.

In the movies, these intimate moments usually dissolved into a soft fade. He'd never thought about how much pounding had taken place in *When Harry Met Sally.*

Every time he left her apartment, though, he couldn't help the feeling that he was being watched. Once he could have sworn he saw a face leering out of the foliage only to slip back into the bushes. By that point, though, the fatigue had gotten so heavy that that it was a miracle he wasn't hallucinating full-time.

Rain had ordered a couple of medical textbooks online and had taken to poring through them on his lunch hour or whenever he wasn't with Kimmie. Most of the language was over his head, but there were diagrams, well-articulated, super-detailed, and heavily labeled. He thought he was beginning to get a sense for anatomy, a better understanding of the clay.

That he might really have to test it was never entered in the foreground of his mind.

But it was there.

Occasionally he thought he saw someone in the overgrown wild space across from the EpiCo parking lot. A figure, always barely perceptible, never there when he looked again.

Ronnie had stopped coming to work after their after-hours rendezvous in the second-floor bathroom. Rain wasn't sure if he'd flat-out quit, kept calling out sick, or was taking some kind of sabbatical, but he thought he understood. It wasn't like Ronnie could drop a hundred pounds overnight and not have it raise a few eyebrows. He was pretty sure Ronnie would stroll back in next week with a sob story about emergency surgery, ebola, or some last-minute liposuction and never look back. Of course, he might have already taken off for Hollywood.

If anyone noticed the mess on the second floor, they never mentioned it to him.

When he'd gotten home after another epic session with Kimmie, he'd found Decker equally insatiable. His little dog pranced and cavorted around the room, dancing on his hind legs like a madman happy that the rapture has come. Rain slipped the chain lock shut and fed him an incredibly late dinner before feeling guilty for a while.

Feet up, he laid down on the couch to pass out from the afterglow. When sleep didn't take him, he thumbed through his copy of *Netter's Atlas of Human Anatomy*.

*Could* he do it? But that wasn't really the question at this point. He thought he could do almost anything. But would she wake up?

The noise he heard from his bedroom closet startled him out of whatever reverie he'd been feeling. Decker whined, and Rain found himself wondering if his dog's ecstatic prancing hadn't been so much *happy to see you* as *finally you can save me*.

It came again, a wet bump from the other room, and Rain closed the book and raised himself off the couch. He was pretty sure the manual was heavy enough to stun a burglar or stop a bullet, and cranked it back for a swing as he advanced.

"Hello?" he called. It was stupid, but some things are just hard wired.

No one answered. Ronnie didn't fall out of the closet with two hoagies and a bashful grin, and Kimmie didn't jump out of a birthday cake. That those were the two best-case scenarios he could think of was in itself disturbing, and instead the apartment remained silent, bordering on creepy. Decker whined.

Pausing at the threshold to the bedroom, Rain listened. There was a faint crumpling sound from just behind the closet door.

Pushing open the bedroom door with the corner of the textbook, Rain steeled himself for attack. There were no more noises, but it wasn't like he could just yell "Case closed!" and drift off back to sleep. Taking a deep breath, he drew back the textbook and threw open the closet door.

Nothing. Just the usual shirts, old boxes—

Something exploded from the top shelf, hitting him like a cannonball and driving him down onto the wooden floor. The textbook went flying from his hand and skidded off under the bed. Rain got his arms up in a pathetic defense, but by then whatever it was had already charged out of the bedroom.

Decker was barking like he'd lost his mind. Rain stumbled to his feet, aware of the bloody patches spreading on his shirt. He didn't feel hurt, but adrenaline was supposed to numb the pain, wasn't it? Had he been stabbed? Was he bleeding out?

Stumbling out into the main room, Rain looked at the front door. What he saw led him staggering onto the couch. For a long moment he could only watch as his mind struggled to process the scene taking place.

It was hopping at the door, a small humanoid in a bloody t-shirt. Little glistening appendages waved furiously above what he assumed must be its shoulders, tugging at the knob and trying to yank it backwards. Frustrated yelps poured from the thing as it put all the strength it had into the effort, little legs heaving, back straining, but the door could only open a few inches.

*It can't reach the chain. It doesn't know that you have to slip the chain.*

*Sweet mercy, it's stuck in here with me.*

For one of the admittedly many times in his life, Rain had no idea what to do. As in most of those moments, he went and got a beer.

The meat puppet struggled valiantly at the threshold for a while, unwilling to surrender this obviously lost cause. Rain recognized the t-shirt as one of his and wrote it off. At least it was an old one.

"Hey," he tried. "It's not going to open."

The homunculus hissed at him and only yanked harder.

"No, really. You've got to slip the chain to open it."

It looked up at the small steel links clearly out of reach, hissed, and gave the door a final yank before turning around, small shoulders slumped in defeat.

There was nothing quite as awful as a sad meat puppet.

Rain checked his shoulders. It actually hadn't cut him. He was a little soppy from its juices, but otherwise none the worse for wear.

The homunculus didn't approach, but hung its head. A muffled mewling sound began to seep from the round ball on its shoulders.

*Oh no. It's crying.*

Weighing his options, he sighed. It wasn't trying to hurt him, although it had probably tried to kill Ronnie. Was it really that dangerous?

"Hey," he tried. The meat puppet looked up.

"If I let you out, you're not going to hurt anyone, are you?"

Its little head wobbled from side to side.

*Do you really think this thing understands you?*

Maybe it was the brutal fatigue or the beer, but for some reason he did. "Why did you go after Ronnie?"

The homunculus paused, tilting the little round ball on its shoulders towards the ceiling for a moment. Satisfied, it turned to the door and traced a pattern with one quivering appendage.

Craning his head, Rain tried to get a better look. Red wet letters stained the wood.

*CN B ONY 1.*

"What?"

Raising its appendages in front of it, the meat puppet put them together and nodded vigorously. When it drew them apart, it shook the round ball from side to side.

"Being apart sucks. You want to be together?" It nodded, and Rain thought about this for a moment. He wasn't surprised to find his beer empty. "Well, he kind of made a choice, buddy."

That mewling sound began again. Rain tried to harden his heart. What he was about to do was almost certainly something he'd regret later, but right now sleep deprivation and pity were allowing him some temporary insanity. "I'll fix the door for you, but you have to promise to stay away from him, okay?"

The meat puppet stood there for almost a full minute until the mewling sound stopped. Finally it nodded the little round ball on its shoulders up and down.

"I mean it," Rain intoned sternly.

It gestured again. Wary of any sudden moves, Rain

cautiously went to the door and drew the chain back. He wasn't really going through with this, was he?

"Here," he said. He pulled an old Portland Peppers cap off of the hook next to the door and set it down on the diminutive puppet's ball. "At least you'll be a little more incognito."

The homunculus nodded again and touched the little green hat before trotting out into the hallway. No one was there to watch him go as he found the staircase door, jiggled the handle, and disappeared from view.

Beginning to accept that he now might never get any sleep, Rain went to the kitchen and popped open another beer while he texted a brief warning to Ronnie.

*Amigo. Puppet dropped by my place. Keep an eye out.*
*Seemed pissed about your breakup.*

He thought about it for a while, and then added:

*He promised to leave you alone. Hope everything's cool.*

That settled, he leaned back onto the couch and flipped open *Netter's Atlas of Human Anatomy.* Decker had just settled down, curling into a little ball by his lap when he heard a soft squishing settle by the front door.

Rain yawned, shook his head, and tried to go back to a diagram of the human respiratory system, but then it came again. He stood, shuffled back to the threshold, and ogled the hallway through the peephole. Nothing.

But the soft sound repeated itself gently. Sighing, he undid the chain and pulled open the door.

The meat puppet stood there shaking, green cap low on its little round head. It stepped past him and slunk back into the apartment.

Rain did a double take to make sure none of the neighbors had noticed and shut the door behind it. Decker's ears had perked up from his position on the couch, but at least he wasn't barking. The dog observed the homunculus with clinical suspicion, which wasn't terrible. Rain had been worried that Decker might eat it.

"What happened?" he asked.

It shifted its weight from one foot to the other and back again. Finally, it took that hat off, held it in one appendage, and traced more characters on the door.

*COLD.*

"What?" But it was no use feigning outrage. The meat puppet looked pathetic as it folded its hat between its paws. He glanced over at the door. Brown juices were already drying against the wood. They were going to need to figure out a method of communication that didn't require Lysol.

The homunculus tilted the little round ball on its shoulders up to Rain and let out a submissive hiss. He sighed and gestured to the corner of the main room. "There's a dog crate I bought for Deck that he refuses to use. It's yours for the night if you want it."

Nodding, the meat puppet padded off to the corner, opened the wire mesh grate, and slipped inside. With paternal irregularity Rain found himself oddly touched when it pulled the dog blanket over itself, rolled onto its side, and lay still.

*What the hell is happening?*


From the chair in the corner of Room 38, Rain snuck glances at his aunt as he pored through *Anatomy and Physiology for Dummies*. It was a little lighter than Netter, but the diagrams were solid and at least the text was a bit more manageable.

By now his aunt hadn't spoken to him in weeks. She was still lying prone beneath the faded blue sheets, machines chirping away, respirator wheezing. He was a little worried that she wasn't going to be able to hold on, that it would take her before he—

But he wasn't sure yet. Not one hundred percent, and he needed to be. This wasn't molding wrinkles or fixing Ronnie's dick. He would be rebuilding the human respiratory system. He needed to be prepared for anything. And he just wasn't there.

*If not now, when?*

He pushed the nagging thought aside. A light rain had begun to patter on the window outside. When his phone vibrated, he glanced down.

Kimmie had been sending him more pictures, almost one every thirty minutes since he'd gotten off work. He appreciated them, appreciated being thought of, but between every cutesy statement was a curt appraisal that killed a little bit of the mood.

*Miss you!*

*Can't wait to feel your hands again.*

*Look at this, cowboy. Do you think one nipple is bigger than the other?*

To be fair, he did study the pictures, but he couldn't tell. He was getting pretty confident that the flaws she kept finding weren't real, but it didn't matter. He was in the middle of his own romance, and if the price of that was a little pointless body modification here and there, he was more than willing to pay it.

When he'd left for work that morning, the meat puppet had still been snoozing away in the old dog crate. When he'd gone back to the apartment to feed Decker, though, the homunculus had been gone. Also gone were three pounds of ground beef he'd been keeping in the pull-out freezer beneath the fridge, the bloodstained plastic-wrapping torn and shredded across the linoleum.

He hadn't thought about this before. *Was it eating?*

Rain had washed the sheet from the dog crate, wet and more than a little brown, and began to dread where it might have wandered off to.

He really hoped it wasn't going to kill Ronnie. As pathetic as the creature was, he didn't think he could live with that.

There was a light knock on the door before Masami slipped inside. Rain nodded to her and she returned it, going through her routine, checking machinery and readings, his aunt's tubes and wires. After a few minutes, she was headed for the door when she gave him a smile. "You going to take my job?"

"What?" Rain glanced down at the anatomy textbook. "Oh. No."

"Just a little light reading?" Her eyes were teasing.

"Just broadening my horizons, I guess."

"Mmm-hmm." Masami surveyed him. "Maybe you should be broadening your nap times. You look great, but you also look like shit. Does that make sense?"

"I've been pretty busy lately."

"What's her name?" When he balked, she smiled again. "I've seen you checking your messages, that little blush you get. It's cute."

Rain grinned sheepishly. "Kimmie."

"Oh, dear. With an 'e'?"

"Maybe."

"Didn't your aunt ever tell you? Avoid people who add an *e* to the ends of their names."

"She skipped that part." Rain found himself smiling.

"Don't worry. I can cut her eyes out when she hurts you."

"My hero."

Masami turned to leave, and the question leapt to his lips. "Hey?"

She turned. "What's up?"

"If you could change just one thing about your appearance, what would it be?"

Her smile faded, just for a second. "Really? Nothing. This is who I am."

When the automatic door slid open, Rain didn't quite run. He was going to get drenched, after all, and no amount of undignified jogging was going to change that.

The deluge made him wish he had reneged and parked in the hospital's garage that day, but he'd found public parking on the street in front of Cosmic Monkey four streets over and thought it was a damn sight better than being accosted again. He'd even kidded himself into thinking the walk might do him good, but the storm made all of the little bonuses he'd dreamed up moot.

Rain made it to the first light and crossed, wary of the headlights around him, the thick freshets of water that cut off visibility and made everything just a tad more dangerous. He'd lived in town long enough to see some pretty gnarly things happen when the rainy season started back up again, and didn't want to be on the receiving end of any of them.

He made it to the second block, crossed at the stop sign, and set off to the east. The street lights in this older part of town were a sodium orange, a strange muted color that didn't illuminate so much as cast creepy shadows for ambiance. The hour wasn't that late, though, and most of the shops and storefronts still had their lights on even if they weren't entirely open.

By the time he reached the fourth block, he was soaked. Pausing at the crosswalk and waiting his turn, he was conscious of the pounding sideways shower and the encroaching cold knifing into his legs and shirt. This last jaunt was the longest, a three-block stretch uphill through one of the city's more historic thoroughfares, and he was imagining the warmth and safety of his Nissan when he spotted them.

They were parked across from the old Hollywood Theater's marquee and in front of Tony's, a black SUV with tinted windows that might as well have had *ABDUCTION VEHICLE* painted on the side of it. A man with a blue suit leaned against the bumper, umbrella spread open above him. He was sipping from an oversized plastic soda cup and checking his phone.

Rain started across the crosswalk, signals be damned, and almost got clipped by an old VW camper van. It let out an enraged *blat* on its horn, and the man in the blue suit looked up.

Their eyes met. The stranger smiled and turned his head to bark something into the car.

Another man got out and followed his associate's gaze across the street, their suits almost a perfect match. The second man waved.

Panic flooded Rain's nerves. Despite the overwhelming urge to get to his Nissan and flee, a small and angry part of him wanted to go over there.

*Let's settle a few questions. Keeping in mind that I literally melted the last one of you who fucked with me, who the fuck are you? And what do you want?*

The light changed, and Rain spared a glance back as he hurried across the walk and up the hill. They weren't coming after him. For now it seemed they were only content to watch. And wait.

He had a sickening feeling the time would come. Something inside him was very sure about that.


She opened the door for him and did a double-take. Rain wasn't positive, but he thought Kimmie was toying with the idea of closing it on him. "What the hell happened to you?"

Granted, he looked more than a bit of a mess. His clothes were still ultra-damp from the walk back to his car and his hair was plastered to his skull. Worse yet was the wild look in his eyes, the panic in his system not quite back to baseline. Rain had toyed with the idea of not coming, of calling the whole thing off, but then again she was his girl. If they were going to make this work, she could see him under slightly sub-optimal conditions.

After a glance in the Nissan's mirror, though, he had entertained some second thoughts. He'd tried listening to the radio, but all that was playing was country or a news bulletin about a deli robbery at the local Kroger and he turned it off. His heart was still hammering away at his ribs.

The callous indifference of that pompous little wave the man in the blue suit had tossed him was lodged like a bullet at the base of his skull.

*Hey there, buddy. Don't mind us.*

"Come inside," Kimmie said. He slunk through the door gratefully and pulled up a chair at the dinette table. She got him a beer from the fridge and quickly threw together a drink for herself from the components on the counter.

Beneath the soft white glow of the overhead light, in the kitchen she looked like an angel. It was silly to get so sappy about it, but Rain was having a hell of a night, and even in a t-shirt and jeans the perfection of her form was stunning, every curve exquisite, every proportion at its maximum potential.

He'd done a hell of a job, if he did say so himself.

Kimmie sat across from him, her face unlined and unreadable, and slid the beer over to him. When she asked again, everything poured out: the assailant in the garage, the man in the blue suit, the subsequent watchers he'd felt or seen. He felt like he was being set up for something, some inevitable ruin, and his surveyors were now inclined to just monitor the situation until the time was right. The not knowing was driving him crazy.

She didn't respond right away, only taking a long slow sip from her tumbler. "So you killed a guy."

"I don't know. Maybe."

"What do you mean, maybe? You said you turned him into human bisque."

"No one ever found him. At least, no one ever mentioned finding him. Maybe it's not permanent."

That last part was a lie. He hadn't done any maintenance work, but his muscles hadn't gone away and it had been weeks. Once he molded flesh, he was pretty confident that it didn't just rubber back. That he had inadvertently created a sentient being out of Ronnie's spare parts, though—

"Really?" There was something in her eyes that Rain

83

couldn't quite read. "What makes you say that?"

"Nothing," He drank a sip of his beer. Sweet, sweet pine tar. "I'm pretty sure it's permanent. It just hasn't been that long since I started doing this."

Her shoulders settled. Had she been holding her breath? "Okay. What are you going to do about it?"

"What?"

"These guys. The blue guys."

"I don't know."

"I mean, if they're watching you they need you for something. They're not going to just kill you."

"Who knows? Right now they may just need me dead in a box."

"Don't say it like that. Jeez." She finished her drink and set it down on the table. "Enough foreplay. Time to get you out of those wet clothes and into something more comfortable. Like me."

Kimmie kicked the kitchen chair back and lifted her shirt over her head. It had been her opening gambit for a while now, and her breasts were perfectly sculpted, her skin a smooth marble. He really had done good work.

"Hold on." That the sight of Kimmie's naked breasts hadn't rendered conscious thought impossible was a new development. "My head's still really spinning here."

"Then you need something to take your mind off of it." She pushed his chair back and straddled him, pressing herself against his wet chest and shivering. "Chilly. Take it off."

"Just give me a second—"

Kimmie put his hands on his shoulders, daring him to swoop lower. "I was looking in the mirror today, and I noticed this little *thing* right here." She traced his fingers along the hollow of her collarbone. "It's like a little rough patch of skin. Can you get it off? I'll be extra nice to you."

He couldn't even see what she was talking about. Maybe it was the damp clothes, or the pounding headache, or chemical afterglow of fear, but he wasn't responding in the traditional way. "Kimmie—"

She dropped his hands to her breasts. "Come on, Hank. Help your goddess."

Rain struggled and then rose, pushing her gently off of him until they both stood awkwardly in the dinette. Once more he had a weird feeling about the stark whiteness of apartment, the lack of photos or personal effects. "I need time to think right now, okay? My head's in a thousand places at once."

"It only needs to be right here." Kimmie crossed her arms over her chest and gave him her best pouty look. It did nothing for him.

"I just can't right now, okay?"

"Then will you at least fix it? I've got this one other thing I saw too—"

Pieces were fitting together in front of his eyes. It was not a comfortable experience.

"I've got to go."

"Can't you fix it first?"

"I can't."

"You mean you won't." The pouty look was gone. Replacing it was a sharper, angrier Kimmie he didn't think he'd ever seen before. "Then get the fuck out."

He laughed. It was hollow in the blank apartment. "Really?"

"Yeah, really. Last chance. You've never had it this good, and when you think about it you'll call. You'll cry, begging to help me out again. You know you can't quit me. Quit your *goddess*."

"Kimmie. After all—" He shook his head. "We had a connection."

"Is that what you thought?" She smiled like a set of knives.

"Don't do this."

"We had an arrangement, Rainier. You help me, and I

fuck you better than you've ever been fucked in your entire life. It's simple. But it's never going to be anything more." She took a deep breath, some of the anger gone from her eyes. In a way, that made it worse. ""You can change me all you want. It still doesn't change who you are."

"Fuck you." He shook his head, trying to clear it, but whatever she'd seen in his eyes sent her retreating behind the counter.

She fumbled in a drawer and came up holding a small, neat handgun. "No take backs. Get out."

Eyes widening, he shook his head and tried to say something. Kimmie took aim with dead eyes, and instead he settled for stumbling out the front door.


Like many people before him, Rain had absolutely no idea what to do next. It was already getting late but he had a sinking surety that he would be using one of his last sick days tomorrow.

Head spinning, he followed his ancestral memories and went to a bar.

Despite the stupid ache in his chest, or perhaps because of it, already the plan was crystallizing. Frantically he was trying to work out the nuances. He was going to fix her. What was left to lose?

He'd been to this bar a few times, usually at several of the down points in his existence. It wasn't flashy and it certainly wasn't upscale, but it also lacked roaches and weekly stabbings. Pleasantly dingy, it was a neighborhood hangout where no one knew your name but could kind of recognize your face and get your drink order right on the second try.

It occupied the first floor of what might have been a small mercantile in the twenties, with a back porch and space for playing cornhole out back. Better yet, the unusual layout had left plenty of booths, nooks, and crannies and people had a tendency to leave you alone. That last part, Rain thought, sounded perfect.

He grabbed a stool at the wall-length bar and tried to remember whatever the hell beer he'd been drinking for the last couple of weeks, Pine Tar probably was probably not featured on the beer list.

"Do you have any IPAs?" he asked the bartender, reasonably sure that this was a good starting-off point to finding his beer.

She was an amiable punk with full sleeves, the sides of her head shaved to stubble. Nodding, she rattled off five or six products that didn't ring a bell.

He tried again. "Do you have anything that tastes like I'm drinking a tree?"

"Coming right up."

As she went over to the taps, Rain turned on his stool and surveyed the bar. It was strange, but that feeling of being watched was creeping over him again.

Smiling, she returned with a pint glass of golden-brown liquid. "Are you going to be here a while?"

Rain shrugged. "Probably."

"Do you want to give me your phone?"

"What?"

She gave him a wry, pitying smile. "The worst thing you can do right now is try to call her."

Stunned, he slipped it across the bar to her. "Are you psychic?"

"Yeah. All us psychics tend bar on weeknights." The bartender made his phone disappear. "It's 11:30, and you've got that look about you. Trust me. Best move you can possibly make."

Rain nodded his thanks, paid for his beer, and sequestered himself at a corner table for some heavy brooding. *How had he let this happen?* was his first thought, followed by the slightly less charitable *She used me!* with the ever-popular *I can still get her back!* bringing up the rear.

How would Hugh Grant have handled this?

None of these thoughts were helping or particularly

insightful, so he tried the beer. It was dank and hoppy, and overall tasted like he was consuming a higher class of foliage. The bartender had made a solid call.

What had he thought was going on between them? Like a barely-glimpsed dream, he couldn't quite figure it out. They'd had a one night stand that he'd tried to stretch out into something more, which in hindsight seemed the plot of a movie that couldn't get Julia Roberts onboard. Maybe there had been nothing there besides pheromones and alcohol. Maybe it had been his mistake to try to carve it into a relationship.

But in the end, he'd had something she wanted. Had quid pro quo been the entirety of her interest in him? Besides the guilt at initially wiping her face into a tabula rasa, had he mistaken her interest for affection? Her greed for lust?

Maybe. Maybe none of those things. All he knew is that he still wanted her, right up until that image of her pointing the little black pistol at him came back, her eyes dead and empty. Everything fell into place.

At that moment, he knew, all she'd been worried about was that he'd try to take it back.

It wasn't like Rain was an innocent party. He'd lined right up and kept molding to keep it going. If he hadn't been sexually drowning, he would have realized it a long time ago.

The lack of intimate details or emotional vulnerability or even conversation had pointed to something destined to remain surface-level. From fucking to fixing to everything in between, all it had been about from the beginning was flesh.

He'd had another beer, staring darkly at a small framed picture on the wall. It was of a small boy in Norman Rockwell pajamas, creeping around the side of his bed at nighttime. His stuffed teddy bear waited patiently on the other side. The caption beneath it read *No One Gets Out Alive*.

"Hey, stranger."

The voice was familiar, and he glanced up. For a moment he didn't recognize her without the scrubs. She wore a cute dress, black unzipped hoodie pulled over her shoulders in a practical sexy-but-not-freezing look. Beneath the fine dark stubble on her scalp, her emerald eyes glinted in the low light.

When he looked up, Masami recoiled momentarily before recovering. "Shit. Bad night?"

"I've had better." He gestured vaguely at the chair across from him. "Are you here alone? Damn, I'm sorry, that sounded really creepy. I mean, do you want to sit—"

"Shut up. And yeah." She sat across from him, a narrow cocktail glass in hand. Rain didn't think he could take the weight of her appraisal. "Girl trouble?"

"The final round, yeah." He sighed and tried not to bang his head off of the table. "For the best, probably. It's just stupid how this never gets any easier. You'd think with all the reps you'd develop some kind of a callus or something."

"Want to talk about it? I've been told I'm naturally empathetic."

"No. Maybe." The bartender set another glass down in front of Rain and raised an eyebrow before hurrying back. Rain nodded his thanks. "I mean, I used her, she used me. When there's nothing below that—at the first scrape, there's nothing left."

"I've been there." Masami gave him a battle-weary smile. "The last person I was with faked me out for about a month or so. When we were together, everything was super intense. Promises of devotion, I'll-do-anything-yadda-yadda. Of course, it turned out all my calls were going to a burner phone. Married with no intention of giving their husband up, not that that was an alternative once I found out. Big talker, only because it was a fantasy she was getting to live out. There was nothing beneath it."

"Shit. I'm sorry." Rain said. He wondered if there was a follow-up question he should be asking, but just let the silence hang for itself.

"Don't be. Pity about yours, though. Why are the pretty ones always insane?" She caught him looking. "You're not as discreet as you think you are with that phone. Trust me, I might have seen more of your girl than you did."

He laughed. It sounded weird to him, in contrast to everything he felt, but it came out anyway. "What are you doing out so late?"

"Again, I'm going to chalk that up to emotional fatigue making you sound creepier than you should. I work swing. I'm out late a lot, not to mention that I've got a day off tomorrow."

"Anything crazy going on?"

"No big plans." She smiled. "I hate to leave you low, but I've got to split. Cats and such to feed. Yeah, I'm one of *them*. Nice seeing you outside of the antiseptic tank, even in these shitty conditions."

"It's good to see you too." His emotions were warring, flaring, sending out false everything. Rain contented himself with shutting up.

She finished her drink and set it down on the table, the faintest hint of lipstick adorning the rim. Masami clapped him on the shoulder. "Buck up, cowboy. Three billion more of them out there. Seven if you'd just broaden your horizons."

"Speaking of which." She leaned over and whispered it to him. "You've got an admirer. And he's sitting in the booth in the back."

Rain looked up and tried to peer through the darkness as she left. There was indeed a figure, skulking in an ill-lit alcove on the opposite side of the bar.

In the gloom he could just make out the green baseball cap, pulled down low over his watcher's face.

*No. He's so much bigger.*

He thought of Ronnie not returning his texts, and a fresh chill sped through his heart. The meat puppet, if it was him, was now the size of a fourteen-year-old boy, a teenager just getting ready for his final run at adulthood. Its round head was still a featureless motley of ground beef hidden beneath the cap and low light. If no one had tried to oust him from the bar, it was because you let people who looked like they lost a fight with a meat grinder sit wherever the hell they pleased.

It twitched nervously at having been spotted, rose to leave, and almost walked into the far wall. Spinning around, it tried to nonchalantly saunter past his table, the bulky trench coat it was wearing already stained at the seams. Rain wasn't thrilled to see it was wearing another one of his t-shirts.

Without breaking stride, the homunculus casually dropped a piece of paper on the table with a hiss. It was out the door before Rain could even form the thought.

*It's twice the size it was yesterday. How is that even—*

The bartender brought him another beer, wrinkling her nose at the trench coated figure as it stalked off into the night. "Was that guy bothering you?"

"No. Old acquaintance, actually." She raised an eyebrow, but he didn't follow it up. He handed her cash. "Can I get my phone back? I think I'm drinking this and heading out."

The punk nodded, and Rain turned over the stained piece of paper. It was a yellow takeout menu for a Chinese restaurant he'd never heard of, mottled with brown characters that took up most of the page. He held it up to the light. A confession or a ransom note seemed like the top two possibilities.

*SRY I*
*8 YR FOD*
*SAD DY*
*FEL LOST*
*WNT STR*
*8 8 8*
*WHER RONNIE?*
*WNT SA HI*
*WNT LTS*
*C U AT HM*

He read it over twice. A twinge of guilt stabbed between

his ribs, quickly alleviated by the alarming knowledge that the homunculus seems to have found a way to consistently break into his apartment.

Rain read it again.

*8 8 8.*

Ate Ate Ate.

He wasn't sure how the meat puppet could physically eat without a discernible mouth or any digestive system, but it had doubled in size since he had seen it last. If it could somehow absorb more meat, more mass—

An image of a ground beef giant, stomping cars into tin cans, flitted through his imagination.

He hurried out to the Nissan, a little worried for Decker. What if the homunculus had lost control? Harmed others? Despite his paternal instinct towards it, he realized that he had no idea what the limits of such a thing might be. He needed to start figuring it out before everything got well and truly fucked.

At least Ronnie was probably okay. He texted him again, a growing unease beginning to take hold. He hadn't heard from him for days, and it wasn't like him to completely drop off the radar.

Speeding home, he reached his building, parked on the street, and hurried in, taking the stairs two at a time. The door was still locked, and once he was inside Decker wagged his tail faithfully at his master's return.

Of the meat puppet there was no sign.


It was finally time.

Rain had called out from work and slept in, spending most of the afternoon reading and consulting the medical textbooks he'd bought. Reviewing diagrams and ticking off lists in his head, for the first time he felt sure that he could do this. Now that the moment had come, though, he felt unbelievably shaky, a little chilled in the antiseptic atmosphere of his aunt's hospital room.

An autumn shower drummed against the windowpane, streetlights streaked orange blobs against the darkness. Thoughts of Kimmie and the gun flitted through his head, and he had to push them away. This had nothing to do with her.

He looked down at his Aunt Lucy, compressed now into this shriveled form beneath the light blue sheets. Memories of her from his childhood came racing back, the strong woman who'd taken a crying kid into her arms at the hospital, who'd stood up in court and said she'd take him in. The little arguments, the minor victories. The love she'd shown him even when he was being a little shit. The furious scolding he'd taken when she found half a pack of cigarettes wadded up in his sock drawer, so pissed and afraid that he was going to get caught up in the vice she hated herself for. The joy she'd shown at his high school graduation, that she'd done the impossible and raised someone else's little guy against all odds into a semi-responsible adult. The happy tears when he'd gotten a place of his own and finally moved out.

The doctors had said that she was out of options and almost out of time. Any minute now could be her last. But they didn't know.

There was always an alternative.

The machines chirped and wheezed behind her like mechanical sentries. Rain leaned down and kissed her forehead for the last time.

Could he do it? He thought so. And the look in her eyes when she finally awoke—

Rain rested his hands across her thin collarbone. Her skin was cold. He thought he might be crying.

With a deep breath, he concentrated. His fingers caught fire.

The agony licked at his tendons, whipping bright pain all the way back to his elbows. With a sigh he slipped his fingers beneath her skin, beneath the subcutaneous tissue, beneath the muscle, until he found what he was looking for.

It didn't want to leave. He could feel that, a black grainy thing like tar, could feel it resisting him, digging in. Rain called to mind the textbooks he'd read, the diagrams he'd memorized. A picture was forming clearly in his head, a purity of form without the lurking pitch of this thing inside her. Slowly things began to take shape.

It warned him. He was sure of it.

His power ground against its edges, and it seemed to buck and growl. It would not be expelled, this obsidian thing that had rooted itself to her lungs. What kind of horror went gently into the light?

Rain began to pull, the pyretic fury in his forearms needling up the pain into true suffering. The first black tendrils began to trickle upwards from the holes dug by his fingers.

Sweat poured down his face. He was animating the tissue, molding it, but in some kind of spiritual feedback loop he realized he was animating the cancer inside her as well, giving it power. Out of everything he'd read, he'd expected this to feel like a medical procedure. What he was encountering felt like an exorcism.

It didn't matter. This was all that was left, all he could do.

Rain's breaths came in harsh pants. He buckled down and yanked harder, a clean picture of the respiratory system in his mind. Her very flesh was now rejecting the black mass, sending it kicking and screaming upward. Gooey tendrils began to stretch, marking the ceiling in nightmare deja vu.

At the end, it wrenched itself downwards, like a drowning swimmer trying to hold on. At the base of his skull, he thought he heard a voice, begging and pleading and beseeching him to stop. The machines chirped louder, quicker, and he knew he had to finish before someone found him, someone burst into the room and saw this horror sprouting from his aunt like a grotesquely overgrown bloom.

The voice gained clarity before it happened. One

buzzing sentence, bursting through the mental static and chilling Rain to the bone. He tried to put it back then, take it all back, but by then it was too late.

*If we can't have her—*

*No one will.*

The dark mass sprouted from his aunt all at once, a great black pincushion of flesh and blades that burst through her chest with a rotten tear. Gobbets of meat and bone flew as her torso exploded outwards in a shower of hot blood that took Rain in the face and sent him skidding to the floor.

His hands began to cool. *No no no—*

The thing raised itself from between her cracked ribs, dangling from the ceiling on obscene tendrils. It was formless, a cascading, rippling mass of darkness that changed shape a dozen times in the half second it took to slip free of her ruined lungs. Bits of gore dripped from its black form as it shook what was left of his aunt loose like an old shoe. The machinery attached to her began to blare, a cacophony of alarm that drowned out all thought, all action.

Selecting a form, it lowered itself to the floor, a liquid black skeleton, impossibly thin, and raised a razored finger beneath Rain's chin.

*You wanted us out?*

The door burst open behind him, and he heard the screams begin.


The third floor of the hospital erupted.

The first person who entered through the door came behind him at a sprint only to let out a muffled squawk as they glimpsed the necrotic horror. They immediately tried to change direction on the tile, slipped, and skidded onto their ass, kicking Rain in the kidneys with one sensible shoe as they tried to find their footing. Someone behind the first began shouting for help, for orderlies, for security, but Rain never saw them. They disappeared back beyond the threshold in an instant, leaving him with the cancerous skeleton and whatever unlucky soul had faltered first.

The night nurse who'd kicked him wasn't entirely unfamiliar, someone Rain had spotted maybe a dozen or so times on the hall. She pushed herself back into a crouch without seeing Rain and tried to pivot on her heel for the door, a pretty athletic move that unfortunately wasn't quite fast enough. The black mass lurched forward, seizing her by the back of the head and pitching her headlong through the opening.

Rain heard a sickening crunch as the night nurse connected with the wall across the corridor. He tried to grab for the monstrosity. If he could just take hold of it, mold it, he thought, like the meat puppet maybe he could make it stop.

*Oh, Lucy,* he thought. *I'm so sorry. I'm so so sorry.*

For something so recently called to earth, it was quick. It seemed to sense his intent, dancing around his clenching hands and scrambling out into the hallway. Screams that had begun in earnest tripled when the dark form lurched into sight.

Rain stumbled to his feet, blood streaming from a gash in his forehead, and propelled himself after it. His ankle had folded strangely when he went down, and now it was a lump of agony with every step.

Two orderlies in white scrubs who were charging down the hall stumbled and fell almost at its feet in an effort to hit the brakes. They were too close, and the creature slammed them together with impossibly sharp fingers, sending freshets of blood cascading across the corridor. The impact almost cut them in half.

A nurse dove behind his station. Another locked themselves swiftly into a closet. A security guard ducked into the nearest room and slammed the door.

The black mass flowed with liquid grace to the fallen woman, her head cracked and bleeding like an undercooked egg. She moaned, and it clamped its long hand noisily around her face. Her skin began to turn an ashen grey, loosening and sagging. The thing's arm began to buck and swell.

*Holy shit,* Rain thought. *It's feeding.*

He looked down the hall. More than twenty doors were cracked or closed, and he thought of the meat puppet. *There will be no stopping it. If it finishes here, no chance at all.*

The security guard popped out of the room, service pistol aimed. Rain barely had time to duck back inside before it roared in the small space, licking fire. Several rounds passed through the thing's wiry frame with as much effect as hitting target paper. Several more struck the nurse. One tore her face into a red ruin.

The creature looked down at her limp body, its face a writhing black cloud of features, and tossed the night nurse down in disgust. The security guard threw the door shut as the black horror streamed down the hall towards him.

A male nurse with close-cropped blonde hair stepped out from around the nurses' station corner and hit it full in the chops with a fire extinguisher. The shot was hard enough to make the cords stand out on his linebacker arms, and had the thing been human, it would have caved its skull in. As it was, the liquid skeleton staggered and lost a step.

Alarms were blaring in an endless chorus of the damned. The hallway smelled of cleaning fluid, blood, and piss. Rain tried to warn the hero with the extinguisher to run, but it was too late. Wordless, the thing took him by the jaw in an elongated hand and thrust him upwards, ramming him headfirst through the ceiling with a terrible *crack*. The man's feet kicked through a cascade of blood for a moment, pawing the air with frenzied steps before he sagged, buried to the shoulders. With a hiss, the thing went after the woman behind the counter.

The stairwell door burst open. Without surprise, Rain saw one of the men in blue suits stumble out. He took one look, recoiled, and shouted something into his phone, panic making his voice high and reedy. He shouted once more as he freed a pistol from his jacket pocket.

The thing sensed if not danger then livelier prey, and ignored the nurse to flow after the newcomer. Rain staggered after it, almost feeling bad for him.

The man in the blue suit opened fire, deafeningly loud in the small space despite the already raucous alarms. Black moons appeared in the wall behind it, and one of the fleeing staff screamed and fell, clutching their shoulder, blue scrubs already going crimson.

"Stop!" Rain's voice was choked, and in the ringing and the smoke he wasn't even sure he was making words anymore.

But the black skeleton pivoted with liquid grace, a rippling at its core that he realized with sickening surety was laughter. *Oh no. We will never stop, father. We are SO HUNGRY.*

The man in the blue suit was reloading. To his credit, he hadn't turned and run when he had the chance. Rain thought he could hear footsteps, other people coming up the stairs, and blindly wondered if there were reinforcements on the way.

If there were, they would get here too late. The black skeleton flicked a razored palm downwards and took the man's hand off at the wrist. The pistol clattered against the floor, a pale pink spider scuttling behind it. The man in the blue suit shrieked, high and piercing, before it took him in its arms.

The bell of the elevator rang, the thin chime somehow audible over the chaotic din. The doors slid open at the end of the hall.

Against all odds the meat puppet sprang onto the corridor, round ball on its shoulders surveying the damage from beneath its green cap. It had grown again, now the size of a college athlete. One of Rain's stained t-shirts hung off its torso, impossibly stretched, and he saw that it was wearing an old garbage bag as a pair of pants. With a hiss, it propelled itself down the hallway, leaving wet brown footprints in its wake.

Enveloping its prey, the black skeleton was swelling, liquid tendrils cavorting and rising around it. Its back was to the elevator.

The black mass never saw him coming.

The homunculus tackled it at a full sprint, the force of it driving both of them into the near wall with a sloppy grunt. What was left of the man with the gun sagged to the floor in a muddy ruin as the meat puppet wrapped its beefy arms around the black skeleton in a crushing bear hug. In turn the grotesque mass wrapped razor fingers around its new adversary, only to draw him closer. They stumbled and waltzed, bouncing off the walls in a writhing frenzy, each struggling for purchase and the upper hand.

Rain felt a new kind of energy, felt it pouring off both of them in waves. At their edges they began to blur, lose definition. Pink bled into black, black bled into pink, and he just had time to think *They're eating each other. Absorbing each other—*

Even after everything else, the explosion was deafening.

The meaty cloud burst with a roar, drenching the halls in brown blood and black meat. Rain went back on his ass in the onrush of gore, covering his eyes with one arm as a grotesque hot rain pattered around him.

The alarms continued to scream, a whooping howl that had long since lost all meaning. Somehow it had all become background noise, and in the resulting chaos Rain stumbled to his feet.

The formerly white corridor looked as if someone had nuked an abattoir. In the center, a red-black smear covered the walls and ceiling in a twenty-foot radius of pure splatter. Hundreds of pounds of shredded meat were strewn across the floor or embedded in the walls. Bodies lay sprawled up and down the hallway without any signs of life.

*Like matter and anti-matter,* Rain thought. He found one of the larger chunks of beef and picked it up. Black veins had crystallized within it, a coruscating infection that had reached its end.

*Inert.* He dropped it in a hurry.

Why the meat puppet had come to his aid was beyond him. Had they shared some bond between the creator and created? A goodwill towards the man who had freed it? He had a feeling he might never understand, but the puppet was gone now. The two had cancelled each other out completely.

He turned back to his aunt's room, but then he heard the footsteps, closer now on the east stairwell. With a sinking feeling of loss and a grief just now beginning to show its true depths, he ran for the exit.

Rain burst out onto the dark street from the west emergency exit. It was only sprinkling a little by then, a shadow of the storm that had raged the night before, but clouds of mist against the streetlights were disorienting. It took him a moment to get his bearings.

He couldn't tell if anyone was following him, but in the moment he didn't care. Ignoring the first stoplight almost entirely, he rushed across the walk, narrowly dodging a pickup whose horn let him know all about it. The second light was run through with the same coin-flip attitude towards survival, and then he was heading east and away from the hospital, out of any would-be pursuer's line of sight.

The hillside began to slope up and away from him, and Rain slowed his pace to a fast walk. He was a lot of things, but swift wasn't one of them, and his breathing was already beginning to hitch, the stitch in his side cutting deeper. His ankle was a throbbing lump of agony.

*Can I just fix it? Expand my lung capacity to store more oxygen? Hell, while I'm at it I may as well get faster, too. If the body's a machine, it's just a question of finding the right specs—*

He halted. The grief hit him between the eyes like a sledgehammer. The last time he'd tried to alter anything he'd killed his aunt and five people who'd gone to work that day to save lives.

Maybe it was time to stop. Maybe it was time to accept

that there was no safe purpose for what he could do, that every time he used it people got hurt. Maybe—

With a screech of brakes and the smell of burning rubber, the white van threw itself up onto the sidewalk ahead, narrowly missing him while clipping a plastic bus stop bench. It skidded to a halt inches from a brick storefront, and Rain froze, bewildered, wondering if this was a chance to redeem himself. Maybe he could heal the driver—

Those thoughts sheared off in a hurry as the panel door flung itself open. Three men in blue suits spilled out, fanning to either side as another leapt out of the passenger seat up front. The latter was either in charge or just liked to yell, and he started barking orders.

Rain was already running before the man could finish his sentence, gimping for all he was worth. All four had identical black pistols, and it didn't take a genius to figure out that their time for watching and waiting was up.

Sprinting over the hill towards his Nissan, Rain gasped for breath. Hard soles slapped against the wet pavement behind him, and Rain waited for the sharp crack of gunfire, the burning impact of a slug as it burrowed its way into his neck. Part of him wanted to just lay down and take it, a penance for the carnage he'd wrought on his poor aunt. The other cajoled him relentlessly onwards.

*They won't kill you. They* can't *kill you. But what they have planned will be so much worse—*

The impact struck him in the small of his back, sending him and the other man toppling onto the sidewalk. The man in the blue suit was quicker, back on his feet with a practiced roll in the time it took Rain to get onto his knees. He got behind Rain and shoved him down with one hard elbow, driving him face first against the pavement. His knee dug into Rain's back as he hollered something to the men behind him. More footsteps were coming now, and Rain could hear the rough engine of the van.

Flailing, Rain managed to get a grip on the stranger's ankle, digging his fingers in just between where the cuff of the man's pants met his sock. Thoughts were eclipsed by instinct, riding over him in a napalm wave.

To an onlooker it would have seemed that the man in the blue suit's knee had suddenly dislocated. It buckled, and the man's weight was suddenly gone, but Rain didn't stop there. Bone became plasma, the man's legs suddenly rubber balloons of meat and blood. He toppled to the sidewalk, howling, his useless legs twitching in feeble kicks.

His friend sidestepped him and delivered a punch square to the back of Rain's neck. White stars danced at the corners of Rain's vision, and he threw a hand behind him, more by chance than anything else colliding with the bridge of the man's nose. The cartilage expanded, flattened, the man's forehead running like putty, and the stranger stopped, raking at his face with manicured nails.

Rain stole a glance as he took off running again. He'd taken the man's eyes.

Bolts of pain shot up from his ankle. The entire foot was a swollen mess, and he wasn't sure he could trust it to hold his weight for much longer. Footsteps pounded on the damp concrete behind him, and in the moment Rain knew he couldn't outrun them. But he could make them pay.

Waiting until they were almost upon him, Rain spun around when he felt fingers grasp his jacket. The last two had reached him at almost an identical time, hands outstretched to drive him down to the sidewalk and end this madness. He seized each of their hands and pushed.

Their skulls distended and became conical, black sunglasses sliding off and clattering to the ground. Both men began to scream as tissue bent, cheekbones melted, and Rain thrust them together with a wet crunch.

They couldn't chase him if they were fused together.

Numb to the wailing, to the carnage he'd caused, Rain

turned and limped up the hill towards his Nissan. The van following him had slowed to a stop. Evidently there were things that eclipsed getting a paycheck.

Behind him someone begged him to fix them. Someone begged him to stop.

He would do neither.


Rain burst into his apartment and went straight for his bedroom closet, yanking out the black duffel bag from the top shelf and throwing it onto the bed. His ankle slid sideways and he almost toppled to the floor, but managed to correct himself with only a lance of agony to show for it. Decker barked and pranced, a happy waltz at his master's return, and Rain rubbed him behind the ears absently as he threw clothes and necessities into the bag.

A number of items still smelled of brown juice and ground beef. It was something Rain was just going to have to live with.

They would be coming for him soon. Either the blue suits or the cops or both. Someone would have noticed that the whole hospital incident had started in his aunt's room, and whatever way he tried to spin it the fact remained that he'd been the last person seen with her before—

He tried not to think of Aunt Lucy and couldn't, couldn't stop seeing her torn to bloody rags by the black thing that lumbered forth. The weight on his chest was almost paralyzing. Hot tears rushed down his cheeks, and he finished packing as quickly as he could and went to the bathroom.

The medicine cabinet had Tylenol and ibuprofen, but nothing that would really help the level of pain that his foot was in. Rain took three of each, figuring his liver was the least of his problems right now, and headed to the kitchen.

He was in the middle of bagging Decker's kibble and treats when the phone went off in his pocket. Rain had been so deep inside his own head he almost hadn't recognized the sound.

No one should be calling him.

With a focused dread, he looked at the screen. It was Kimmie's number. He hadn't thought to take her picture down.

Everything ground to a crawl. His hand was a glacier as he took the call. "Kim?"

"Rain? Oh, thank you thank you thank you. Rain!" Almost panting, her voice had a high hysterical quality that turned Rain's nerves to glass. "These men, they broke— they took me—they want you—"

Her voice cut off. For a moment, the line went dead, and then a male voice spoke, gravelly as a pit. "We've got your other friend too. Looks like that guy in the Conan movie. Do you ever want to see them again?"

Cold fear shot up his spine. He tried to lean against the counter and instead just managed to slump against it."Yes."

"Good." There was another long pause. Kimmie shrieked something in the background. "You understand that I'm a little pissed at you, right?"

"I don't know who you are."

Another pause. "Fair enough. Go to your door."

"Who are you? What do you want with me?"

"That doesn't matter right now. Go to your door."

Rain managed to stand, the ankle shrieking. He gimped over to the apartment door. "Okay."

"Open it. Strawberry."

"What?"

"Open it."

He did as he was told. There was a paper lunch bag sitting at the center of the threshold.

"What is this?"

"Open the bag."

Looking deeper into the hallway, he couldn't see anyone. It was if the paper sack had materialized in the last five minutes.

He picked it up and sorted through the contents. There was a small bottle of fluid and a hypodermic needle.

"Do you see the bottle?"

Rain allowed that he did.

"Open it. You're going to inject yourself with three milliliters. Don't be a dipshit, strawberry, and blow an air bubble into your vein."

"I don't think so."

The voice on the other end of the phone sighed. "Then your friends are dead. And I'll still send people after you. How many carny freaks do you think you can leave behind before the feds get involved?"

Rain had no answer to that. The needle felt very heavy in his hand. "What do you want from me?"

"There'll be time for that later. Plenty of time. Look, I'm going to need you to take action here."

"What is it you want?"

"Kid, I'm going to give you sixty seconds to do what you're told. Then I'm going to start cutting your lady friend's fingers off." Kimmie shrieked indistinctly in the background, and the man's voice came back on. "Fifty."

Thoughts whirled through his mind. His first selfish instinct was to just go. To hell with all of them, he could just skip town and disappear. His life here was over anyways.

The weight of it pressed down on his chest. He'd already horribly failed today. He couldn't do it again.

"Forty."

Rain cracked the seal of the bottle and flipped the plastic cap off the syringe. "Where am I supposed to stick myself?"

"What?"

"I've never done this before. Is there some kind of approved technique? Will just anywhere work?"

There was a muffled exchange on the other end of the line. The man with the gravelly voice came back on. "Leg. Stick yourself in the top of your leg."

"Through the pants?"

"What? Of course not. Are you trying to get me to send

someone up there? So you can melt them into a fish monster or something?"

"Why a fish monster?"

"What?"

"It just seems like a very specific pull."

"Shut up. Twenty seconds."

Filling the syringe, Rain dropped his pants and jabbed himself. There was surprisingly little blood or pain as he depressed the plunger, only the sinking sensation that he might not have entirely thought this through. Placing the syringe on the coffee table, he yanked his pants back up and collapsed onto the couch. Already the ceiling was drifting away, receding into a faint pinprick of light.

His last thought before he drifted off was realizing that he'd locked the door.

# BONE

The rush of cold water jolted Rain awake.

Sputtering, he tried to move his arms and couldn't. He had to wait for the water to run from his face, shaking his head as best as he was able to.

Rain was in a concrete room with a high ceiling, maybe twenty feet by thirty. A steel door with a ramp zigzagging down at the far end was the only discernible exit. It was cold but not freezing, probably because he was now dripping wet.

He was in an uncomfortable chair that had been bolted to the floor. His wrists were cuffed by steel bracelets to either arm, and duct tape had wrapped his shins to the front two legs.

To the right, a man in a blue suit with close-cropped hair had poised the second bucket of water to throw. When they made eye contact, he set it back down on the unfinished floor. He looked slightly disappointed that Rain had come around.

To the left, an older man with a salt-and-pepper grey beard was dressed in an immaculate black suit. Vitality radiated off of him like cheap cologne. A small director's chair sat between him and the other man. He glanced over at his colleague and shook his head. "Dave, are you really going to take that bucket of water out of here?"

Dave shrugged.

"You went through the trouble of standing at the sink, filling the bucket, dribbling it on in here, and getting it on your shoes. It doesn't matter if he's awake. Just throw it on him, okay?"

"Okay." Dave picked up the bucket and sloshed another gallon or so onto Rain, who coughed and spluttered again.

"There." The bearded man turned his full attention onto him. It was like being under a spotlight.

Rain coughed out a mouthful of water. "Who are you?"

The bearded man shrugged. "I bet you have a lot of questions. I do too. But as I am not currently tied to a chair, I think I'll start."

"What do you want me to change?"

The man in the black suit nodded. Dave wound up and punched him across the face. Between the stars and the bolt of pain, Rain realized he was wearing gloves.

"I said I'll ask the questions, okay? Don't be strawberry rude." The bearded man straightened his tie. "You know what? I'll tip my cards a little. Ever since that little lady from the hospital tipped us off, I've had people watching you. Some of the things you're supposed to have done—I mean, ew. So, my first question: how sick a fuck are you?"

"What?"

Dave raised a gloved fist, but the other man waved him back. "That one's a freebie, Dave. See, I meant to get a rise out of him."

To Rain, the bearded man nodded. "Those guys. The mugger in the garage. My friend Manuelo. Those security tapes didn't come cheap. Neither did cleaning up after you. Why didn't you just kill them?"

It took a second for Rain to process what he was saying. A hard lump grew in his stomach and threatened to sink him beneath the floor. "Are you saying they're not dead?"

A blur of motion, and then another bright bolt of pain.

Rain could taste the blood seeping out of his nose. "Don't answer a question with a question. Rude." The man in black looked over his shoulder and nodded.

The steel door at the far end of the room opened. A man in a white coat pushed a two-level aluminum cart down the ramp. On the first table was a plastic tub. On the second was a cage the size of a grocery cart basket.

Rain recognized the two occupants. The human soup and the ball of flesh began to rock back and forth, slightly agitated.

"They had a lot to say about you, once we settled on a mode of communication. Believe me, that was the hard part. I mean, they don't have mouths any more, per se, or eyes, or really anything. Hank here can't even explain how they're still alive. Can you, Hank?"

The white coat looked nervously over at Dave. "No. I mean, from the MRIs they don't even have distinct organs—"

"Can it, Hank." The bearded man turned back to him. "They told me everything they knew, so I promised them I'd ask. Can you put them back together?"

"No."

The man in black *tssked*. "Well, at least I tried. Are you sure?"

"Yes."

"Strawberry it. Take them down to the incinerator, Hank."

The liquid man and the human ball began to slightly froth and gyrate. Without a word, the man in the white coat wheeled them away. Rain thought he was going to be sick. He hadn't known.

But after the meat puppet, couldn't he have guessed?

"Ugly business, kid." The bearded man looked him in the eye. "You really didn't know? Good for you. Because otherwise that's some pretty fucked up shit. If I could melt another person into lobster bisque, I guess I would also make the not-radical assumption that they were dead."

"So you know that we know. It's been established that you have this crazy fucking power. Can you guess what comes next?"

"You want something."

"Hey, fast learner. You're right. I need you to take something out of my head."

Rain took a stuffy breath. At least most of the bleeding had stopped.

"I don't want to get hit." Out of the corner of his eye, he saw Dave raise his fist, so he hurried on. "But I don't think I can. I think you know what happened at the hospital. That was me trying to remove something."

For a moment, he thought Dave was going to hit him anyway. The bearded man tutted thoughtfully. "I respect your concern. When you do your thing, things tend to get really hot tacos. Let me spell this out for you."

He nodded at the door again. A man in a blue suit opened it and brought in a black leather briefcase. He placed it on the director's chair and popped it open. Green bills lay banded together in neat rows.

The bearded man gave the newcomer a curious look. "Scott, what is this?"

"One hundred thousand dollars."

"Why'd you open it?"

The newcomer shrugged and eyed the ceiling. "You know. To show him that you mean business."

"He's tied to a strawberry chair, Scott. You could have brought in an empty briefcase. A briefcase full of phone books. A briefcase full of gummy bears. It's a goddamn p—forget it."

The bearded man turned back to Rain. "What he said. In cash. In addition to my assurance that we will not only take any and all measures to ensure that the hospital situation does not replay itself here, you and your friend get to walk out of here."

"Friend?"

The blow was immediate, a solid shot to his temple that sent white lights spinning around the concrete walls.

"Friends. I meant to say friends." The bearded man didn't look very convincing.

"If you're just making a business proposition, why all the guns?" Rain raised his palms to ward off the next punch, but it never came.

"Rainier, I'm going to be straight with you. Obviously, I am a man of some resources. With an inoperable brain tumor pressing down on my against my prefrontal cortex and putting terrible pressure on my baseal gland, it would be foolhardy to not employ what resources I have. Is that a fair assessment?"

When he didn't respond, the bearded man just shook his head. "Let me be blunt. I'm twelve months into having six months to live. Even the time I'm taking to tell you this is borrowed. If your answer is no, I'm going to take your friend apart with a chainsaw before I start in on you in the hopes that I might change your mind. I might drop dead in the middle of it, but since this is my last chance those are odds I'm willing to take."

"You said friend again. Singular."

"No, I didn't." The bearded man looked wounded for a moment, and then sighed. "Fine. Friend singular. Bring her in here."

He nodded to the door again. Rain felt a familiar sinking feeling penetrate his stomach as Kimmie walked in, looking none the worse for wear. She'd even put on a cute dress for the occasion.

"After you melted a vanful of my guys, I thought I'd change direction. Thankfully, your friend here had already approached one of my blue boys. In hindsight, you probably shouldn't have mentioned them." The bearded man shrugged in a kind of what-can-you-do gesture. "The fake hostage call has already cost me two grand, plus the caveat that you do a little more forced labor for her benefit. What can I say? She's a tough negotiator."

It was as if someone had dropped an anvil on his solar

plexus. Rain couldn't speak, could hardly breathe.

"So, yeah, friend singular. She's probably going to be hanging out here for a while. Nice work, by the way. It's always good to meet another connoisseur."

"Let me see Ronnie." Rain's voice sounded choked and pathetic, even to him.

"The Hawaiian looking guy? No. That would have been a great condition if I didn't already have you shackled to a chair, though."

"I've seen your face. Scott and Dave, too."

"What, are you an expert on strawberry faces now? Jeez, no wonder she dumped you. Trust issues, am I right?"

Kimmie shrugged, and Rain felt his panic beginning to rise.

"What if you have another growth? A blood clot? Are you going to find the *other* flesh molder? You're never letting me out of here." He caught Kimmie's gaze. *Jerry Maguire* hadn't ended like *Saw 6*, had it? "Kimmie, they're going to kill me."

Kimmie shrugged, her cute dress wrinkling around her perfect shoulders. "I made you a better offer, Rain. Now I've got to take what I can get."

"Really?" He struggled to find the words. "It meant nothing to you?"

"Nothing personal. You'd done everything you were willing to do. I still needed more."

"I'll do whatever you want. Just get me out of here."

She looked bored. "You'll do that anyway before they're through."

Dave chuckled. "I think he's going to cry."

"Rude, Dave. Fucking rude." The bearded man looked at his watch. "Ten minutes. Have your answer or I'll show you what's left of your friend."


After the others had left the room, Rain was left with Dave, a briefcase full of money, and ten minutes.

It wasn't a lot of time to sort out the questions that kept jostling about for primacy. Neither did it help that Dave stood a comfortable distance away with his pistol pointed in his direction. There was no way he could mold himself to slip out of the bindings without the man in the blue suit putting one through his kneecaps.

Could he do it again? Raise a black horror that would tear through the population like wet taffy? Was it worth it if he could save himself?

And Ronnie, if they actually had him. He hadn't seen him or spoken to him, though it explained a lot about why none of his texts had been returned. It wasn't Ronnie's fault he was in this mess, but the point would be moot if he tore the dark thing out of the bearded man and it murdered them all.

Either way, he was pretty sure he would never leave this room. You didn't go to all this trouble to abduct someone only to let them leave and promise not to call the cops. The briefcase was a prop, or had been meant to be. An incentive to appeal to his greedy side, to give him a positive he could lie to himself over.

The bearded man knew the negatives of what Rain could do. And he could never take the chance that Rain could put the thing back in.

"Dave?"

The man in the blue suit looked up from his phone. "Yeah?"

"Do you really have Ronnie?"

"The Conan looking motherfucker? Yeah. Kind of pointless to say we're going to carve him up if he's not here."

Rain nodded. "He said that you had taken precautions? Against something like what happened at the hospital?"

"Flamethrowers." Dave didn't look up from his phone. "At least two."

"Who the fuck are you guys?"

"That'll never concern you. You're in a disposable room

113

in a disposable building. Do what you're told."

"And leave? Do what I'm told and leave?"

"Sure." It wasn't particularly convincing.

"How many of you are there?"

"Enough."

"What happened to the guys in the van?"

The man in the blue suit sighed. "What do you think?"

And it all clicked into place for Rain. The barest sliver of a plan emerged dripping from the primordial muck. He knew what he had to do.

Dave slipped his phone back into his pocket. "Look, I don't like you. You did some really horrible things to the people I work with. I'd rather not play twenty questions. In fact, I'd rather you outright refuse. I've never taken a chainsaw to someone before, and you've got a lot of hurt coming to you. It'd be a shame if no one collected."

"Tell him I'll do it."


With some trepidation, they unlocked the cuffs before Dave scattered back to the head of the room. It had been too long and his fingers were cold sausages. Rain took a deep breath and flexed his hands, willing some of the feeling in them to return.

Stomach fluttering, he found it hard to concentrate. So much was riding on the next five minutes.

The men in blue suits stood around him in a rough triangle. Rain was a little surprised to see that three of them actually did have flamethrowers, something he'd seen in action films but thought was pretty much a complete myth in real life. They'd set themselves up each at hundred and twenty degrees of the circle, which was smarter than he'd given them credit for. In theory, they could roast him alive and not have to worry about melting each other's faces off.

The director's chair had been shoved back almost to the door. Dave paced the room in front of it. He hadn't been gifted with a flamethrower, but had his pistol out in one hand and was rubbing his temples with the other.

"Settle down," Rain said. "I'm sure he'll be here."

The man in the blue suit shot him a dirty look. "Fuck off or I'll put one in your knee."

Rain shut up.

The door at the far end of the room opened and the man in the black suit walked down the ramp. There was a bounce in his step, a jaunty little hop that didn't speak to hostages or emergency surgery.

"So," the bearded man said. "Are we going to do this?"

"As long as the deal's the same. The hundred *k*," Rain said. "And Ronnie and I walk."

"Of course, of course." The bearded man didn't try to sell it in the least. "So what do I have to do here?"

"You weren't at the hospital. Are you sure these are enough guys?"

"It's what we've got. These guys don't exactly stand around in front of the Home Depot."

"Aren't they going to toast me when this thing comes out of you?"

"No, no, no." It was a strange way to pronounce *I don't give a shit*.

Rain sighed. None of it mattered. There was only one way to move now. "Come over here. I've got to put my hands on you."

"Sounds kind of tent revival." The man in the black suit crossed the room. "Just so you're aware, and this is a standard caveat, Dave will fill you full of holes if you fuck around on this. I don't want to come out of this looking like a fish monster or some kind of strawberry platypus. Do we have an understanding?"

"Yeah." The bearded man was standing in front of him, but Rain couldn't quite reach his face. "Can you get down?"

"What, like kneel down before you? No. I'm not doing that."

Rain felt the first itches of frustration as the tips of his fingers heated up. "Well, it's that or let me out of the chair. I need to be able to touch your head."

The bearded man nodded. Dave approached, tugging a pocket knife from his pants pocket. He snapped the blade to full extension and cut through the tape on Rain's legs with the practiced ease of a butcher. Rain only had a moment to be surprised that it had been that easy before blood rushed back in his limbs in an excruciating flood of needles.

"You okay there, friend?"

"Yeah. I just couldn't feel my legs. Give me a minute."

"No. Dave?"

Dave gripped him by the armpits and yanked him to his feet. The flood of agony as he put weight back on his wounded ankle made him cry out, and the man in the blue suit shook his head in disgust.

"Like I said, we're short on time. Let's do this."

Rain made a show of stretching, marking where each man was, and hobbled a step forward, placing his palms on the bearded man's temples. He felt the familiar burning sensation return, the pain rip up his arms, driving pins into the base of his skull. There was one way out of this, if he could be quick.

He began to feel throughout the bearded man. The muscle, the bone, the skin, the black mass squatting at the base of his skull. Rain did some quick calculations. There should be enough. Just enough.

"Hot tacos. That shit hurts." The bearded man gritted his teeth and grunted. "Take it out, kid. Get it all out."

The burning sensation escalated into a pyre. His marrow felt like molten silver. For a moment Rain was afraid that he'd pass out, that all of this would have been hilariously pointless, and then he steadied himself.

Meeting the bearded man's eyes, the words came out in a whisper. "You know I can't do this."

"What?"

And Rain pulled.

It happened in an instant. The bearded man seemed to collapse inwards from the feet up, limbs hollowing into red balloons as everything caved in towards his skull in a grotesque singularity. Four growths exploded from his liquefied head in hard ropy tendrils, shooting outwards like points on a compass. Rain saw the first two strike home, punching through the foreheads of two flamethrower holders like rotten fruit. One whistled over past his shoulder and he heard the man scream.

Dave was faster than he'd given him credit for, dodging the fourth before Rain could whip it back and rip his throat out, but he was firing the pistol by then. Hot metal tore through Rain's abdomen, his chest.

There was nothing left to do, Rain thought as he collapsed.

But become undone.


The lights were out.

Warm, sluggish thoughts rippled outwards like waves in a pool. In the vestigial darkness, Rain found himself drifting.

Formless.

Hopeless in the void.

Infinite and present.

This is how things could be, forever.

He dreamt.

Not of events, not of people, but soft colors. Warm feelings. Pastiches of emotion, rendered down to their core shades.

It was primordial, without fear or desire or need. He was, and would simply continue to be until he wasn't.

Time passed. He had lost the ability to calculate it, or the depth to care. Everything for him was the instant. Everything for him was *now*.

And then a thought appeared, wholly different from the others.

*You were once human.*

It wasn't comforting. Quite the opposite.

But it persisted.

It hurt. There were memories, dark places, a sense of purpose. Guilt. Pain. Needs, each more fractal and convoluted than the next. He could see the vague outline of a form, diagrams and concepts but also another sense of the whole, an elusive being so much different than what he was now.

A figure that he had once been, one that caused him so much pain.

With a trembling tendril, he touched it.


When Rain congealed back into a person, the ceiling was on fire.

He patted himself down, not quite believing that he was now bareass standing in a room full of gore. There were no marks, no wounds. Had the oozing soup really been a dream? Would he ever be sure?

Bits of ash and black dust cascaded from above him in a filthy shower. Smoke had begun to fill the room in a choking stench. The problem, he saw, was that one of the blue suits had managed to depress the trigger of the flamethrower as he fell backward, sending a jet of propane blue flame coruscating towards the cheap ceiling. Everything had taken its natural course from there.

He looked down at what was left of the bearded man, now a spoked human wheel. He wasn't much more than a skull with four massive protuberances jutting out fifteen feet or more. It was some of his best work, and the idea that the bearded man might still be alive troubled him not at all.

Judging from the roof, it would only be for a few minutes more.

Dave had bled out at the foot of the director's chair, that troublesome little pistol still clutched in a bloody hand.

Above him was the briefcase, full of little green paper that Rain eventually recognized.

His thoughts were still off, some of them troubling and alien. He wondered if that would ever fully go away.

Taking the briefcase, he opened the door and walked into a short hallway. He turned, opened another door, and walked through what looked like a small break room of short tables and chairs into another corridor. Picking a direction at random, he went left down the longer chamber, opening side doors as he went.

He found a small locker room and put on one of the white coats and scrubs hanging from a series of hooks, which left him looking like a medical-grade flasher. Already the building was beginning to fill with smoke.

There was no sign of Kimmie. Ronnie, either. Rain wondered if they'd ever had him to start with.

The last door opened onto a concrete loading dock. As Rain walked up the long driveway to the road, flames were already beginning to lick at the sky.

With a roar, the black van came slaloming around the corner, skidding to a halt at the top of the dock and cutting Rain off from the road.

The familiar burning sensation coursed through Rain's fingers, a burst of flaring agony that was in its own way enjoyable. As the door flew open, he prepared to ruin.

Ronnie hopped out from behind the wheel, his Hawaiian shirt billowing in the wind. A baseball bat dangled from one hand, but when he saw Rain his face changed from vengeful demigod to amazed relief. "Whoa, whoa, amigo!"

Behind him, Decker leapt out onto the pavement and hustled towards his owner. He stopped, no more than twenty feet away, and studied Rain with one fuzzy ear askance. Was Rain's scent different now? Could he put himself completely back together and not expect to come back changed?

"Deck!" Whatever worlds lay between them, this seemed to

close the gap, and the terrier hurried over for mad dances and petting. Rain looked up at Ronnie. "How'd you find me?"

"Those assholes in the suits didn't know who they were dealing with." Ronnie patted a massive bicep. "I mean, sure, lure me in with free sandwiches, but once they drove me over here I broke free and ripped off their van. I swung by your place to see if you were okay, but you weren't there, so I figured I'd check this place out. Real assholes. When they weren't talking about you they kept talking about chainsaws and shit. What are you wearing?"

Rain glanced down at the lab coat. "Some dead guy's things."

"What's in the bag?"

"A hundred grand. Maybe more."

Ronnie's jaw dropped open. "That's some life-changing money, amigo."

"Yeah." Rain looked back at the warehouse. "Let's start over."

The roof was well and truly burning now, an oily black smoke beginning to scar the sky. He let Decker into the back of the van and slipped into the passenger seat as Ronnie got behind the wheel. He didn't know where they were going yet. Wyoming might be nice. Maybe Florida. Hell, Ronnie might even get his shot at Hollywood.

He heard Decker growl from the backseat. At first Rain couldn't see anything, but finally he could make it out by the floorboards in the breaking light.

It was no bigger than a finger, maybe the size of an action figure as it struggled up onto the passenger seat. Its little round ball of a head swiveled towards him, and it raised an armstalk in a sheepish greeting.

Rain slipped it a piece of Decker's jerky. As they took off down the road, it began to feed.

# ABOUT THE AUTHOR

Roland Blackburn is a father and beer afficionado living with his family and three small dogs in Troutdale, Oregon. He's never used sorcery to enhance his appearance. The third arm was a gift.